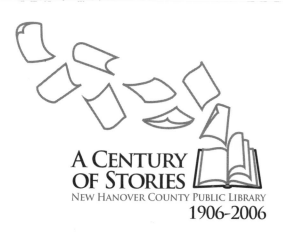

A CENTURY
OF STORIES
NEW HANOVER COUNTY PUBLIC LIBRARY
1906-2006

In Love,

In Lucca

Barbara Cartland

In Love,
In Lucca

THORNDIKE
CHIVERS

This Large Print edition is published by Thorndike Press®, Waterville, Maine USA and by BBC Audiobooks Ltd, Bath, England.

Published in 2006 in the U.S. by arrangement with Cartland Promotions.

Published in 2006 in the U.K. by arrangement with Cartland Promotions.

U.S. Hardcover   0-7862-8832-9   (Romance)
U.K. Hardcover 10: 1 4056 3902 4   (Chivers Large Print)
U.K. Hardcover 13: 978 1 405 63902 6
U.K. Softcover 10: 1 4056 3903 2   (Camden Large Print)
U.K. Softcover 13: 978 1 405 63903 3

The text of this Large Print edition is unabridged.
Other aspects of the book may vary from the original edition.

Set in 16 pt. Plantin by Al Chase.

Printed in the United States on permanent paper.

British Library Cataloguing-in-Publication Data available

Library of Congress Cataloging-in-Publication Data

Cartland, Barbara, 1902–2000.
    In love, in Lucca / by Barbara Cartland.
       p. cm. — (Thorndike Press large print romance)
    ISBN 0-7862-8832-9 (lg. print : hc : alk. paper)
    1. English — Italy — Fiction.   2. Lucca (Italy) — Fiction.
3. Large type books.   I. Title.   II. Series: Thorndike Press
large print romance series.
PR6005.A765I49 2006
823′.912—dc22   2006015037

AUTHOR'S NOTE

I visited Lucca in March 1990 when I was staying in Florence.

I was thrilled by its charm and its extraordinary and perfect four miles of Mediaeval walls built in 1501/1645.

The Cathedral is just as I have described it in this novel and I actually prayed at the Church of St. Francis of Assisi which is also part of my story.

The beauty surrounding Lucca has been put into words by a great many famous poets.

It is a dazzling part of Italy which anyone who visits it will find hard to forget.

It is not surprising that Napoleon made his sister the Princess of Lucca.

Also many of the famous Roman characters and those of The Renaissance were all closely associated with the city.

CHAPTER ONE

Paola burst into the Drawing-Room.

"Mama, Mama, I am back!"

The Countess of Berisforde rose quickly to her feet and held out her arms.

"Darling!" she cried. "I have been waiting for this moment and was so afraid the journey would take longer."

"It was quite long enough," Paola said kissing her Mother. "I would have flown back like a bird if I could."

The Countess laughed.

"It is lovely to have you, my Dearest, and you look very well."

She held her daughter at arm's length, looking at her lovely face, as if she was appraising it.

Then she said seriously:

"I am afraid, my Precious, I have bad news!"

"Bad news, Mama?" Paola exclaimed.

The Countess nodded.

Holding her daughter's hand, she sat down on the sofa and drew her down beside her.

"Papa learned yesterday," she said, "that your Grandmama is dying and he has had to

7

go to Yorkshire to be with her."

"Oh, Mama, I am sorry," Paola said. "Papa will be very upset."

"I am afraid it will upset us all," the Countess answered, "because you realise, my Dearest, we will be in deep mourning until the end of the Summer."

Paola stared at her Mother before she said:

"I never thought of that. You mean, I cannot be presented and go to any of the Balls we planned."

The Countess shook her head.

"I am afraid not. As you know, everything is arranged and I have even bought a number of new dresses for you."

"Oh, Mama, how disappointing!"

There was a note of concern in Paola's voice.

All the plans they had been making so carefully would now have to be set on one side.

At least until the time of mourning was over.

Paola had been eighteen in February, but she had stayed until the end of term at her Finishing School near Bath.

Her Father and Mother did not want her to come to London until the beginning of the Season.

She would then be a *débutante* and attend all the Balls, Receptions and other Festivities.

Now Paola realised with a sinking of her heart that none of that could take place.

However, she was too fond of her parents to say anything that would distress them.

After a moment she said:

"In that case, Mama, I suppose we will go to the country, and at least I can ride Papa's horses. Has he any new ones?"

"I have a better plan than that," her Mother said quietly.

Her daughter looked at her with raised eyebrows.

They were in fact very much alike.

The Countess had been the greatest Beauty of her generation, and Paola resembled her.

There was no doubt, her Mother thought, she would be acclaimed as the most beautiful *débutante* of the Season.

Now, a little hesitantly, as if she was feeling for words, the Countess said:

"I knew, Darling, how disappointed you would be and when an old friend called unexpectedly yesterday, she gave me an idea."

"Who was it, Mama?" Paola asked.

"I do not think you have seen her for years," the Countess replied. "She is the

Contessa Raulo, a distant Cousin of my Mother who, you will remember, was half-Italian. In fact Marta and I were at School together."

Paola was listening, wondering at the same time how this could concern her.

"When I told Marta yesterday how disappointing it was that you could not be presented at Court," the Countess went on, "and that your Father and I could not give the Ball we had planned for you, she made a suggestion which I think will interest you."

"What is it?" Paola asked without much enthusiasm.

"Marta Raulo is returning to Italy in two days' time," the Countess replied, "and she has suggested you might like to go with her."

"To Italy?" Paola exclaimed.

"I think you will find it interesting," the Countess said, "because Marta lives in Lucca, which is a very attractive town in Tuscany."

She paused for a moment before she went on, as if she was looking back into the past.

"I visited Lucca many years ago before I was married to your Father and thought how attractive it was at the foot of the Apuan Alps. It still has its sixteenth century ramparts intact."

"And the *Contessa* has asked me to stay with her there?" Paola said.

"She suggested that you go back with her to her home in Lucca. Then in a month or so you might visit Florence."

Paola's eyes lit up.

"I would love that. I have always longed to see the wonderful Botticelli pictures there and all the others I have read about."

"Then that is what you must do, Dearest," the Countess said. "I cannot bear to think of you moping about in the country, while all your friends are enjoying Balls in London."

"I am sure I would be quite happy, if you were there, Mama," Paola said. "At the same time . . ."

"At the same time," the Countess interrupted, "you will enjoy Italy. It will be a new experience and I am quite certain it will open for you new doors of knowledge of which you have never yet dreamt."

Paola laughed.

"Oh, Mama, that is just the sort of thing you would say, but I feel at the moment I am so crammed with knowledge that I will give myself mental indigestion."

The Countess laughed.

"You must not be too clever! Papa has always said that women who are too clever and keep showing it off are boring."

"That is only because Papa is much cleverer than they are," Paola said. "Of course I am sorry about Grandmama, but she is very old."

The Countess knew this was true.

Her Mother-in-law had been ill for some years.

She had become so senile that she did not recognise the relatives who went to visit her.

"Your Father will arrange everything," she said aloud. "At the same time, it will be difficult to have to wear black all through the Summer, and you know how much I dislike it."

"I dislike it too," Paola said.

"But my Dearest, there will be no need for you to wear black, since it will not be known in Lucca who you are."

Paola looked at her Mother in surprise.

"What do you mean by that?"

"The *Contessa* tells me that she lives a very quiet life and does not entertain extensively. She therefore suggests that you shall stay with her just as Paola Forde, and do not use your title."

Paola looked surprised but the Countess went on:

"I think it is a good idea for several reasons."

Paola waited but her Mother said no more.

"You are hiding something from me, Mama!" she complained. "What is it?"

The Countess laughed.

"I never could keep a secret either from your Father or from you, but this is something a little different."

"What is it?" Paola demanded again.

"Marta Raulo spoke to me of the *Marchese Vittorio di Lucca.*"

"And who is he?" Paola enquired.

"He is actually the most important man in Lucca but he has been behaving somewhat badly and has shocked a great number of people including my friend Marta."

Paola thought for a moment. Then she said:

"I think Mama, that what you are saying is that you do not wish me to meet the *Marchese.*"

"You were always very quick-witted, my darling," the Countess said, "and that is exactly what I am trying to say, only not very tactfully."

"Why do you think," Paola asked, "that if I go to Lucca using my title I would be more likely to meet him?"

The Countess paused for a moment. Then she replied:

"Italians are very conscious of their ancestry, and are exceedingly proud of their Family Tree."

Paola was listening, and the Countess continued:

"My Mother, through her Mother, was related to the Lucca family, and my friend the *Contessa* thought it highly undesirable if the *Marchese* were aware of this and expressed a wish to meet you."

"But I might like to meet him!" Paola teased. "How old is he, Mama?"

The Countess hesitated.

She thought it was a mistake to go on talking about the *Marchese.* Then, as Paola was obviously waiting for a reply she said after a moment:

"He must be getting on for thirty and one way or another he has had a somewhat chequered career. I am sure he is someone whom your Papa would not want to be one of your admirers."

Paola laughed.

"I think you and your friend are fussing unnecessarily. I am sure there are masses of beautiful women in Italy who would be thrilled to meet the *Marchese* who, in consequence, would pay no attention to me."

"He might feel, as you are vaguely connected with his family, that he should invite

14

you to his house. But Dearest, if my friend thinks it would be a mistake I am sure it would be far better for you to interest yourself in the beauties of Lucca and forget about the man who bears its name."

Paola's eyes twinkled.

"I can see, Mama, that you and the *Contessa* are making a real drama out of this. Very well, I will be 'Miss Forde from Nowhere' and will make quite certain that the dashing and apparently naughty *Marchese* sweeps by without noticing me."

"If you are not noticed," the Countess said, "then remember there will be no need for you to wear the ugly black we both dislike. So I have bought you some very pretty new gowns in which you will undoubtedly dazzle the other residents of Lucca."

"I hope so," Paola said, "but I have the feeling, Mama, there is going to be a lot of culture for me to imbibe which of course will be very good for me. And I will come back speaking fluent Italian and demanding pasta at every meal."

The Countess laughed.

"That would certainly be a shock to the staff, and Mrs. Dingle has been planning all your favourite dishes for dinner tonight."

"I must go and see her," Paola said, "and is Nanny upstairs?"

"Yes, of course she is, and very excited at the thought of seeing you again," the Countess replied.

Paola kissed her Mother.

"It is lovely to be back, Mama, and I only wish that I could stay with you, or that you were coming to Italy with me."

"I too wish I could do that," the Countess said, "but perhaps, when mourning is nearly over, and Papa is becoming bored, I could persuade him to pay a visit to Lucca. The *Contessa* has already said she would be delighted to see us both."

"Then that is a promise, Mama," Paola said. "You know I will be counting the days until you join me."

She kissed her Mother again.

Then she ran from the room saying as she went:

"I must see Nanny and, of course, all the other staff who have known me for so many years."

The Countess heard her daughter's footsteps running down the passage and gave a little sigh.

She had so looked forward to bringing Paola out this Season.

She had already accepted on her daughter's behalf several dozen invitations.

She had also been planning the Ball they

would give at their house in Park Lane.

It would undoubtedly be one of the most memorable of the whole Season.

She could not help feeling at the back of her mind that it was very tiresome of the Dowager Countess to die at this particular moment.

Everyone had been expecting her to pass away for the last two years.

Now it meant that the Summer Ball could not take place.

It would have been enhanced by the guests being able to walk in the garden.

Instead Paola must be a winter *débutante* and have a Winter Ball.

Winter Balls, the Countess thought, were never quite so glamorous.

Then she told herself that, whenever it took place, no-one could eclipse, or even equal her daughter's beauty.

She was well aware that Paola would be outstanding amongst the other *débutantes* although there would be many pretty and attractive girls amongst them.

Perhaps it was due to her Italian blood that Paola's beauty was unique compared with her contemporaries.

She in fact resembled the paintings of Botticelli more than any other girl the Countess had ever met.

17

Her hair had the same strange golden-orange tinge.

It was quite unlike what was expected of a fair-haired English girl.

Her eyes had a touch of green flecked with gold.

"She is really beautiful," the Countess said to herself.

Then she felt a little frightened because such beauty could in some ways be dangerous for a young and innocent girl.

However she was sure that her friend Marta had been wise when she said:

"If Paola is going to be as beautiful as you, then it would be wise to keep her out of sight until she can be properly presented at Court and then enjoy herself as a *débutante*."

The way she spoke made the Countess realise that wherever Paola appeared there would be innumerable young men seeking her out.

They would pay her compliments, send her flowers and undoubtedly lay their hearts at her feet.

She was now however, being obliged to move in the shadows.

She would meet eligible bachelors only by chance rather than as a matter of course.

She would not be able to enjoy the wider view of Society in London than that the

18

country could offer.

She would also, the Countess knew, look wrong in black.

The strange Botticelli gold of her hair would be too dramatic framed in crêpe.

That would in itself be a mistake.

"She will be safe in Italy," the Countess told herself.

Paola, having hugged her old Nurse, went down to the Kitchen to shake hands with the Staff.

They were all delighted to see her and exclaimed at how tall she had grown.

They said she was as pretty as her Mother had been and that was saying a great deal.

It was some time before Paola went back to the Drawing-Room.

To her surprise it was to find that her Mother was not alone.

With her was a Cousin, Hugo Forde, whom she had not seen for a long time.

When she entered the room, he stared and exclaimed:

"Goodness! This cannot be the little girl I carried on the front of my horse, who kept complaining I did not go fast enough."

Paola laughed.

"That was years ago and then you disappeared. Where have you been?"

"All over the world," Hugo replied, "and I have enjoyed every minute of it."

"You must tell us all about it," the Countess said. "I am so glad you are back now, in time to see Paola before she leaves for Italy."

"Italy?" Hugo Forde questioned.

He was a good-looking young man of about thirty-five.

Because he had spent a great deal of time in the East, his skin was sun-burnt.

There were also lines on his face which was unusual in a comparatively young man.

"It will not seem very exciting to you," Paola said, "when I know you have been to Tibet and every other strange place in the East. But for me, Lucca at the moment, is 'El Dorado'!"

"Lucca?" Hugo Forde asked, raising his eyebrows. "Why are you going there?"

"Paola is going to stay with my friend, the *Contessa* Raulo," the Countess explained. "I do not know if you have ever met her. She has a charming Villa in Lucca and it will be wonderful for Paola to be able to stay there for the Summer since she cannot take part in any of the festivities of the London Season."

"I must say," Hugo replied, "I thought the old Countess would have died years ago."

"She has been very ill," the Countess replied. "In fact she recognises nobody."

"Well, I have no wish to live to be very old," Hugo said, "and I think anyway it is most unlikely I shall do so."

He laughed as he spoke and the Countess said:

"From what I have heard of your experiences, Hugo, and the dangers you have encountered, I think you have been fortunate to have lived this long!"

Hugo Forde laughed too.

"I have lost count of how many times I have thought, 'This is my last moment on earth,' only to find myself by a miracle still living!"

"You must tell me about it — you must!" Paola begged.

The Countess rose to her feet.

"If you are going to stay with us, Hugo, which I hope you will, I must go and see about your room. And of course your Valet is with you?"

"That is rather a grand word for him," Hugo replied, "but he has followed me faithfully over hill and dale, into gorges which I thought would swallow us up, and through tribal wars in which reluctantly I got involved."

"Of course I remember Jackson," the

21

Countess smiled, "and we will look after him as well as we look after you."

"You were always my favourite relative," Hugo said, "and may I say the most beautiful."

The Countess gave a little laugh.

"Flattery will get you nowhere!" she replied. "At the same time, I will order a bottle of your favourite champagne. I have not forgotten which it is."

"You are wonderful, as you have always been," Hugo Forde replied, "and I assure you, I am very glad to be home."

He opened the door for the Countess.

As she left the room she patted him affectionately on the shoulder.

Hugo Forde came back to Paola and sat down on the sofa beside her.

"Now tell me about yourself," he said.

"All I want to hear about is you," Paola answered. "As yet, I have done nothing exciting, but I hope to have the chance in the future."

"What sort of excitement?" Hugo asked.

"I do not know exactly," Paola said as if she was trying to think, "but I want more in life than *débutante* Balls and proposals of marriage which to my friends at School were the height of their ambition."

"You will get all that and a great deal

more, looking as you do!"

He was looking at her as he spoke.

Because she was very perceptive Paola said:

"What are you thinking about? Tell me. I want to hear it."

"How do you know I was thinking of anything?" Hugo asked.

"You were, were you not?" she persisted.

"Very well," he said. "I am wondering whether I can trust you with something which might be dangerous — then of course it might not!"

"Whatever it is, I would like you to trust me," Paola said. "If it is to do something difficult, all I can say is that I will do my best."

Hugo smiled.

"You are exactly as I thought you would grow up to be," he said. "And may I point out, my beautiful Cousin, it is quite unnecessary for you to have a brain as well as a beautiful face."

"I want to have both," Paola replied. "It may sound greedy, but there is so much that I want to see, hear and feel, that it would be a waste just to sit back and hope people will admire me."

"Of course it would," Hugo agreed, "and now I am going to trust you, although I have a feeling it is something I should not do. At the same time it is impossible for me to refuse what is being offered to me, quite unexpectedly, on a plate."

Paola moved a little closer to him.

"What are you saying?" she asked. "Does it have to do with something that has happened in the East?"

As if instinctively Hugo looked over his shoulder.

Then he lowered his voice as he said:

"I arrived in England yesterday morning and came here, thinking I would be more or less unnoticed amongst my own family."

"And why should you want to be unnoticed?" Paola asked.

"Just for the moment," he said, "I am a marked man."

Paola clasped her hands together.

"But why? Please tell me why?"

There was silence.

Paola knew that Hugo was still debating with himself as to whether he should confide in her or not.

She looked up into his face saying:

"Please, tell me. You know I would never repeat anything you asked me not to. If it is a puzzle you are confronted with, perhaps I could help you solve it."

"You may be able to do that," he replied,

"and now I think about it, it is almost as if Fate had brought me here at this particular moment."

"What particular moment?" Paola asked.

"When you are about to go to Italy," he answered, "and of all unlikely places, to Lucca."

There was such a note of surprise in his voice that Paola stared at him.

Then she asked:

"Why is it so unlikely and what does Lucca mean to you?"

Again Hugo looked over his shoulder. Then he said:

"I have undertaken what has proved to be an extremely dangerous mission on behalf of the *Marchese di Lucca*."

Paola's eyes widened.

It seemed to her extraordinary that once again she was hearing about a man she did not know existed until today.

"It is a long story with which I will not bore you," Hugo began. "But when the *Marchese* was in India, he saved the life of the *Nizam* of Hyderabad. The *Nizam* was extremely grateful and to show his gratitude presented him with a diamond."

"Was it a very valuable one?" Paola asked.

"It is unique," Hugo replied, "and came from the *Nizam*'s own private Diamond

25

Mine. It is the most perfect stone it has ever produced."

"I would love to see it," Paola said.

"That is exactly what you are going to be able to do," Hugo answered, "because I am asking you if secretly, and without anyone being aware of it, you will take with you to Lucca the ring that belongs to the *Marchese*."

Paola stared at him.

"But how is it that you have it?"

"It was stolen from him, and when he was telling me of his loss he offered me a very large sum of money if I would retrieve it for him."

"But how . . . how could he be so . . . careless as to lose it?" Paola enquired.

Hugo smiled.

"I am not certain exactly how they got hold of it, but some very astute and extremely daring thieves stole it, and there was nothing the *Marchese* could do personally to get it back."

"So he left India," Paola said as if she was working out the story for herself, "and asked you if you would try to find it for him."

She thought her relative was hesitating in his reply and she went on:

"I know you have undertaken a great many secret missions, and have played a large part in what Papa told me confidentially is known as the 'Great Game'."

"Your Father should not talk about such things!" Hugo said quickly.

"It was only to me," Paola said. "In fact I doubt if he has even told Mama, but one of his friends was involved in the 'Great Game' and was eventually killed."

"It can be very dangerous," Hugo admitted, "but getting the ring back for the *Marchese* had nothing to do with the 'Great Game.' It is just that, as usual, I am down to my last penny. If you want to know the whole story, he offered me twenty thousand pounds to recover it for him."

Paola gave a cry.

"That is a great deal of money!"

"It certainly is to me," Hugo replied, "and I can assure you I have earned every penny of it."

"By risking your life?" Paola asked.

"Not once, but two or three thousand times," he answered, "but I found it. Now the difficulty is to get it to the *Marchese*."

"Then of course I will take it for you," Paola said.

"It is something I ought not to ask you to do," Hugo said, "but I cannot help feeling that no-one will suspect a young and innocent girl of being involved, while if I take it

27

to Lucca, it is very unlikely I will come back alive."

"Then of course you must stay away, and I will take the ring to the *Marchese* for you."

"Will you really do that?" Hugo asked. "If you do you understand that you must not breathe a word to anyone, not even to your Father or Mother for I know it is something they would forbid."

"No-one shall know — no-one!" Paola vowed. "I am certain that once I get to Lucca it will be easy for me to hand over the ring without anyone being aware that I have done so."

She was thinking as she spoke that the one person her Mother and the *Contessa* had said she was not to meet was the *Marchese*.

'There will be no need for me actually to meet him,' she thought to pacify her conscience. 'Once I am in Lucca there will be a dozen ways by which I can get it to him without being personally involved.'

"How can I tell you how marvellous you are?" Hugo was exclaiming. "I am ashamed of myself for involving you. At the same time I cannot believe, if you are sensible, that you personally will be in any danger."

"Then of course," Paola said with a smile, "I will be very sensible!"

CHAPTER TWO

The *Marchese Vittorio di Lucca* dressed himself quickly and with an expertise which came from years of being self-sufficient.

He was nearly ready when Princess Leone opened her eyes.

"You are not leaving, Vittorio?" she exclaimed.

"It is nearly dawn," the *Marchese* replied.

The Princess sat up in bed.

She was without doubt one of the most beautiful women Florence had ever seen.

She had been compared to the pictures for which the Galleries of Florence were famous.

Her admirers had taken her through the Pitti Palace and the Uffizi Gallery.

They had pointed out her eyebrows in one picture, her lips in another, and her little straight nose in a third.

Now, with her hair falling over her bare shoulders, she could only have been depicted by Leonardo da Vinci or Fra Filippo Lippi.

The *Marchese* however, was concerned with tying his tie in front of the mirror which stood over the fireplace.

"Come and kiss me, Vittorio," the Princess pleaded. "I cannot think why I should have fallen asleep."

"It is not surprising," the *Marchese* answered.

He was thinking that their love-making had been exceedingly fiery.

He had found the Princess one of the most insatiable women he had ever known.

At the same time he now had an urge to leave and was almost impatient to be on his way home.

"When shall I see you again?" the Princess asked.

Her voice was soft and seductive.

She knew that when she used a certain tone men found it irresistible.

"I am not certain what I am doing tonight, or tomorrow," the *Marchese* replied. "When does your husband return?"

"Not until Thursday," the Princess answered. "Oh, Vittorio, we must spend as much time as we can together. We may not have another opportunity for some time."

The *Marchese* understood exactly what she was saying.

He was however, reluctant to be tied down.

He was not certain why.

He had pursued Princess Leone with the determination of an experienced hunter.

She had not been reluctantly captured; very much the opposite.

But her husband was exceedingly jealous and seldom left her unattended.

Now he had been called to Rome by the Pope.

It was an opportunity that neither the Princess nor the *Marchese* had any intention of missing.

"I love you!" the Princess said suddenly with a passionate note in her voice. "I love you, Vittorio, and it is agony to let you leave me. Stay with me a little longer and tell me that you love me too."

It flashed through the *Marchese*'s mind that this conversation should have been at the beginning of the evening.

When the Princess had fallen asleep in his arms he had not been surprised.

But now he knew that he needed the comfort of his own bed for at least a few hours of deep sleep before the day started.

"I will let you know about tomorrow night, Leone," he said.

He moved towards the bed as he spoke.

Princess Leone flung out her arms towards him.

She certainly looked exceedingly beguiling as she did so, and just for a moment the *Marchese* hesitated.

Suddenly the door opened.

The maid-servant who had let the *Marchese* in earlier in the evening when the footmen were no longer on duty put her head inside.

"His Highness, Madam, has returned!" she gasped. "He has come back!"

For a moment the *Marchese* felt as if he was turned to stone.

The Princess, however, threw herself out of the bed and ran across the room.

"Quickly, Vittorio, in here!" she whispered.

Wondering what she was doing, the *Marchese* followed her.

She went to the side of her very elaborate and elegant wardrobe.

It was painted in shades of blue which the Italians admired on their more elaborate furniture.

The handles and catches were painted silver.

Reaching the side of the wardrobe, the Princess opened a panel.

It revealed a space behind it just large enough to hold a man.

There was no need for her to speak.

The *Marchese* stepped into the darkness

and the panel shut behind him.

The Princess, swift as a bird, flew back into the bed.

She pulled the sheets over her.

She had only just put her head on the pillows and shut her eyes when the door burst open.

The Prince came in.

He stood for a moment staring at the bed as if he could not believe what he saw.

Then in a voice of thunder he demanded:

"Where is he? Where is that Devil? I intend to kill him before he can leave my house."

The Princess opened her eyes.

Then in a well simulated tone of surprise she cried:

"Gustavo! You are back! How wonderful! I was not expecting you so soon."

"I know that," the Prince replied through gritted teeth. "Where have you hidden him?"

"Hidden — who?" the Princess asked. "What are you talking about, Gustavo?"

She sat up in bed as she spoke and her husband asked furiously:

"Why are you naked? Why are you not wearing a nightgown?"

The Princess pushed her long hair back from one shoulder.

"It was so hot, and I was not — expecting visitors."

"But *he* was here! I was told he was here!" the Prince roared.

He walked across the room as he spoke and pulled violently at the doors of the wardrobe.

He could see in the light from the candles burning by the bed that there was only the Princess's gowns inside.

They were a kaleidoscope of colour, fluttering a little in the breeze he created as he opened the doors.

The Prince slammed them shut and walked to the window to look behind the curtains.

There was no-one there and again he said furiously:

"He is here! I know he is here!"

"I — do not know what you are — talking about, Gustavo," the Princess murmured.

"You know as well as I do," the Prince said sharply, "that Vittorio di Lucca has been pursuing you, and it is unlikely that he did not make the most of my visit to Rome."

"You are being quite ridiculous," the Princess said. "You know, Gustavo, that I love only you, and that I need no other man in my life."

"I was told that Lucca was here!" the Prince asserted.

"Who told you such a lie?" the Princess enquired. "If you are having me watched, Gustavo, I consider it unkind and deceitful of you."

"It is you who are being deceitful," the Prince argued.

Now his voice was not so aggressive.

But he was still looking round the room as if he was sure the *Marchese* was hiding under a chair or a sofa.

Yet he could not be certain that he had not been deceived.

The Princess held out her arms to him.

"I have not yet welcomed you home," she said softly. "It is lovely to see you, and I have been very lonely since you went away."

"I do not believe you," the Prince said.

At the same time as he looked at his wife his voice softened.

"Go and undress and come to bed," the Princess whispered. "Then I will tell you how glad I am to see you and how much I have missed you."

For a moment the Prince hesitated.

Then he felt there was no point in continuing to accuse her of something he could not prove.

He put the revolver he was carrying into

the pocket of his coat.

"Very well," he said a little gruffly as if ashamed at his own weakness, "but there are a great number of questions I want to ask you before I let you 'pull the wool over my eyes', as you have done before."

"How can you be so unkind and so . . . unbelieving?" the Princess asked tentatively.

"You are too beautiful — that is the long and the short of it!" the Prince said almost as if he was speaking to himself.

He went from the room.

There was the sound of a door opening further along the corridor.

The Princess waited for half a minute before she got swiftly out of the bed and gently closed the door the Prince had left ajar.

She then sped across the room to the wardrobe and opened the secret panel at the side of it.

The *Marchese* stepped out.

As she put her finger to her lips he followed her on tip-toe across the bedroom.

There was another door which led into a narrow passage used only by the servants.

The *Marchese* passed into it and saw at the far end the Princess's special maid who had warned them of the Prince's arrival.

As he joined her she moved without a

word down a steep staircase which led to the back of the Palace.

There was a door which opened into a courtyard.

As the *Marchese* reached it he could not help noticing that the bolts were drawn back.

The key turned in a lock that had been recently oiled.

He pressed a number of gold florins into the woman's hand before he stepped into the courtyard.

On the other side of it there was a gate leading into a dark alley.

The *Marchese* knew his carriage would be waiting in one of the narrow streets on the other side of the Palace.

Not near the front where it could be observed by anyone passing.

Or in this case by the Prince arriving home.

It took the *Marchese* only a short time to locate his vehicle.

As he got into it and the footman shut the door he thought with relief that he had had a narrow escape.

He was well aware of the scandal which would have been caused if the Prince had shot him as he intended.

All Florence would have said it was only what he deserved.

The carriage carried him swiftly back to his own house which was some distance away.

As it did so, the *Marchese* kept wondering how many other men had escaped from the Palace in a similar manner.

He was obviously not the first lover to be hidden behind the secret panel.

Then led down the back stairs by what the French called a *complice d'amour.*

He realised as he listened to the Princess's conversation with her husband how specious she was in convincing him of her innocence.

It was, the *Marchese* thought, very cleverly done.

It must also have been rehearsed a number of times before!

He had not expected the Princess to be as pure as driven snow.

Nor as the most beautiful woman in Florence to be unaware of her attractiveness.

But he could not help feeling it was undignified to have been hidden in what had clearly been a hiding place for other men before him.

He realised how skilfully the Princess had managed to deceive the man whose name she bore.

It was at this moment that he knew he had

no wish to spend any time with her again.

It was not because he was afraid of the Prince's revenge.

In some way he could not explain to himself, the Princess simply no longer attracted him.

The *Marchese* was used to his love-affairs of which there had been many, ending abruptly for one reason or another.

He was usually bored by the repetition and the inevitability of it.

What he disliked now was feeling degraded by the knowledge that he had followed in the footsteps of other lovers.

They had escaped retribution by the same means as he had.

He did not dispute the fact that the Princess was the most beautiful woman to whom he had ever made love.

Yet her conduct and her calmness in the face of danger somehow revolted him.

Suddenly he felt sorry for the Prince because he was genuinely in love with his wife.

And all too easily he was being deceived by her.

'I shall not see her again,' the *Marchese* decided before he reached his house.

It was a magnificent building which overlooked the river.

It had been designed by one of the great

Architects of the Renaissance.

It had been filled with treasures over the years, to which he had added his contribution.

He was well aware how many women were eager to share with him the beauty of his house and his other possessions.

There were many also who loved him without them.

But he preferred to be on his own.

He had no intention, as he had said often enough, of ever marrying again.

He had been married when he was just twenty-one.

It had been arranged by his Father and was considered one of the most important weddings of the year.

His Father had chosen for him the daughter of the Duke of Tuscany.

It had been a triumph for the then *Marchese di Lucca* to be closely affiliated to the Dukedom of Tuscany.

Vittorio had hardly met his wife before the wedding.

She was just seventeen, not at all attractive and heavily built.

She had none of the grace that he associated with the women depicted by the great artist whose pictures surrounded him at every turn.

They had a very grand wedding attended by everyone in Florence.

The marriage was celebrated by His Holiness the Pope.

After hours of eats and drinks the young couple had driven away on their honeymoon.

Vittorio already had a reputation with the Ladies.

He was outstandingly handsome.

Because of his title as well as his looks, there were a number of Florentine Beauties only too willing to teach him the Arts of Love.

Because he was being gossiped about, his Father had hurried him to the altar.

He was afraid of Vittorio making the mistake of running away with some married woman he fancied.

Worse still of marrying beneath him.

The pressure was impossible to resist.

Vittorio had allowed himself to be manipulated into marrying the Duke's daughter.

She came to him with an enormous dowry and some masterpieces of sculpture.

These were, Vittorio's Father thought, exactly what was required to enhance his Villa in Lucca.

Two days after he was married Vittorio knew that he was bored to distraction.

A week later the Bridal Couple returned to Florence.

There were whispers but not too loud, because even the gossips were afraid of the Duke, that Vittorio had taken a mistress two weeks after the wedding ceremony had taken place.

No-one knew if this was true or not.

What was obvious was that while Vittorio was seen everywhere, his wife seldom appeared.

She spent most of her time with her parents at the Palace.

It was easy as the months went by to excuse this because she was bearing Vittorio's child.

She obviously had no wish to be seen in public.

This certainly did not stop her husband from being a guest at every important dinner-party.

And he was seen at every amusement that took place in what was then the most exciting City in Europe.

Nobody except Vittorio knew how trapped he felt and how much he longed for his freedom.

When it came he was actually some distance away in a Villa by the sea.

With him was an exceedingly beautiful

woman whose husband was on a Diplomatic mission to St. Petersburg.

Vittorio received the news that his wife and his unborn child had died in a carriage accident.

It was not a particularly violent one.

But his young wife had been slightly crushed, which had killed the baby and the Doctors had not the skill to save her life.

Vittorio of course appeared at the Funeral.

But all Florence was talking about his love affairs and condemning him for neglecting his wife.

He had no wish to be talked about in such a manner.

Not that it worried him personally but because it upset his Father and Mother.

He set off therefore to travel round the world.

He was away for nearly three years.

When he returned it was to find that his Father had died and he was now the head of the family.

His Mother had returned to Lucca, where she died two years later.

It was then he reiterated what he had said before, that he had no intention of remarrying.

There were a number of male relatives

who could, in the event of his not producing a son, inherit the title.

They could be trusted to care for the possessions that had been so painstakingly collected over the centuries.

When people told him he was making a mistake, he merely laughed.

"As long as I am not tied to one woman and being bored to distraction, I can enjoy life."

It was certainly something he did in his own way.

He did not trouble in the least what people said about him.

He travelled, bringing back more treasures to fill his houses in Lucca and Florence.

He had become far more handsome and distinguished-looking than he was as a young man.

There was not a woman anywhere in the land who would not open her door to him if he wished to come in.

Husbands might grind their teeth with fury, wishing they could kill him.

But it was difficult to reason with a man who laughed at danger.

What was more, who seemed to understand how annoying he must be to other men!

He fought several duels and being an excellent shot, most undeservedly managed to win them all.

He had the best horses and the most experienced Chefs.

His carriages were the envy of everyone whenever he appeared in them.

Nevertheless, he was still bored.

He walked into his house now and went straight up to his bedroom.

He found his man-servant, who had travelled with him since he had started going round the world, waiting for him.

Ugo was an ugly little man with a sense of humour which the *Marchese* found irresistible.

"You are very late, *Signore,*" Ugo said as the *Marchese* entered the bedroom.

"I very nearly came home in pieces, Ugo," the *Marchese* replied.

Ugo held up his hands.

"Not again, Signore? One day you will go too far!"

The Valet helped him out of his evening-coat, and his master walked across the room to pull back the curtains.

The dawn was just appearing in the sky.

There was no wind and it promised later to be a hot day.

"I am bored," the *Marchese* said aloud.

45

"I am bored, Ugo, and I have nothing to do today."

What he was really thinking was that he would certainly not be spending the evening with Leone, and there was nobody else in whom he was interested.

Ugo put his head on one side and after a moment he said:

"Why not go home, Signore? It is a long time since we have been in Lucca."

The *Marchese* turned round.

"You are right, Ugo!" he exclaimed, "it is far too long a time to have spent away from such a delightful place."

He was thinking that at this time of the year his gardens would be filled with flowers.

He could see the fountain that threw its water high into the air, and which he had loved as a boy.

"You are right, Ugo," he repeated. "We will go to Lucca at once. Pack our things and we will leave before luncheon today."

Ugo was all smiles.

This was something he had wanted for a long time.

He was thinking too that it was typical of his Master to be bored so quickly.

Perhaps there would be new adventures to occupy him in Lucca.

46

Almost as if the *Marchese* was following Ugo's thoughts he said:

"I doubt if there will be much to do there except in my mind, and that is a part of my anatomy I have neglected of late!"

Ugo chuckled.

"You will soon find new interests in Lucca, *Signore,*" he said firmly.

"I hope you are right," the *Marchese* answered as he slipped into bed.

As he lay down he knew he was in fact very tired.

It was unusual, but he thought his tiredness was not only physical, but also mental.

Too long had he listened to the chit-chat of women who could speak only of love.

Too long had he gone from dinner-party to Bedroom, and from Bedroom into the chill of the night.

"What do I want? What am I looking for?" he asked himself.

He had a sudden vision into the past of all the women to whom he had made love.

He could see a long line of them like wraiths towards the horizon.

Women! Always women!

Dark, fair, red-headed, loving, exciting, thrilling, until he knew them too well.

Then inevitably came the predictable

47

boredom, when he knew that enough was enough.

"Yet what else is there?" he queried.

He was rich. He could buy anything he wanted.

But what did he want?

He knew if he offered his services in helping to govern Tuscany, he would be welcomed by the Duke.

They always enjoyed having newcomers with new ideas.

But surely in a short time he would find that too an incredible bore.

"I have no wish to rule anybody!" he said as if on the defensive.

It suddenly occurred to him that, if he had a son, he would want to guide him.

Just as he had himself been guided when he was small.

Only when it came to his marriage had his Father failed him.

For some time afterwards he had hated him because it was due to him that he had been trapped.

Fate had rescued him from years of having to listen to the dull conversation of his wife.

He knew that eventually he would not have even bothered to reply.

Even with the thought of having children,

which he knew he would enjoy, he could not bear to think of re-marrying.

"Never! Never!" he told himself as he turned over in bed. "But — there must be something else — something I can do, something I can feel!"

Once again he was thinking of Leone.

How lovely she had looked when he had gone to her that evening.

She had been waiting for him in her Bedroom, just as he had expected.

She had been standing against a large arrangement of flowers.

She looked exactly like one of the statues of goddesses he had in his house in Lucca.

She was wearing a diaphanous nightgown which did not disguise the curves of her exquisite body.

Round her neck was a string of perfect pearls.

For a moment he had stood looking at her as if bewitched.

Then as the maid closed the door softly behind him, he went towards her.

He had thought she was everything he wanted; everything he desired.

"I thought perhaps you would forget to come to me tonight, Vittorio," Leone said in a voice that he could hardly hear.

"I have been counting the minutes until

this moment, when we could be alone," he had replied.

It was not the words that came from his lips that mattered.

It was what he was feeling about her beauty as he savoured the moment when the world would stand still.

It was something he himself experienced, but was never certain if anyone else did.

It was like the calm before the storm.

The darkness before the first hint of light in the East.

It was difficult to breathe.

Then Leone had moved into his arms and her lips were against his.

The *Marchese* turned over in bed.

He did not want to remember — he did not want to recall what he had felt squeezed into that small box behind the wardrobe.

He wanted to be man enough to come out and confront the Prince.

He felt it was despicable to be hiding from anyone.

Let alone the man from whom he had stolen his wife.

But such heroics would only harm Leone.

At the back of his mind he suspected that she had no wish to surrender her title and position as the Prince's wife.

Nor to cause a scandal that would seriously affect her social standing.

Instead of which he had listened to her cajoling her husband.

As he did so he realised that her protestations were merely those of the flesh.

She would not sacrifice any of the things that mattered to her.

Like so many other women before her she wanted to 'have her cake, and eat it'.

As he heard her begging her husband to undress and come to bed, the *Marchese* told himself that he hated her, and all women.

They were cheats, they were coquettes.

When it came to the point, they would take away a man's manhood, and give him little in return.

He had followed the maid down the narrow passage and out into the courtyard at the back of the Palace.

As he went he was telling himself this was nothing to be proud of.

It is something rather degrading and he would never allow such a thing to happen again.

At the same time some voice within him was asking:

"How could you manage? How could you live without love?"

But was this love?

That was the question.

CHAPTER THREE

Paola was awake but had not been called when there was a tap on her Bedroom door.

She thought it must be the maid.

However before she answered, the door opened and Hugo came in.

"I am very early," he said in a low voice, "but I am just leaving."

"Leaving?" Paola questioned.

She sat up in bed pushing back her hair from her eyes.

"Why are you going so early?" she asked.

"I thought it might be dangerous for you if I were seen with you," he answered, "when you are going to Lucca."

Paola stared at him as if she did not understand and he went on:

"I am going to Scotland on the early train to stay with my Uncle and do some salmon fishing. I shall be out of the way, and if anyone is watching me, which I doubt, they will not suspect any connection between us."

Paola smiled.

"It all sounds very 'cloak and dagger'!" she said.

"It is all that and a great deal more,"

Hugo answered. "In fact I have been worrying all night that I ought not to involve you in it."

"Nobody will suspect me of being anything but a tourist," Paola said, "who is enjoying the sights."

"That is what I have been assuring myself," Hugo agreed with satisfaction.

He sat down on the side of her bed and felt in his pocket.

"Keep this somewhere safe," he said, "and for Heaven's sake, do not lose it! I cannot go through that experience a second time."

He paused before he went on:

"By the way, I have written to the *Marchese* a very guarded letter saying that I have done what he asked me to do, and the proof of it will be reaching him in a short time."

"He will be delighted to think you have been so clever," Paola exclaimed.

"All I hope is that he will pay into my Bank the money he promised me," Hugo replied. "I am almost down to my last sixpence!"

Paola laughed.

"I promise you I will be very careful," she said.

Hugo held out a very small package to

her, and when she looked at it she smiled.

He had wrapped the ring in some rough linen, then wound over it several strands of cotton to hold it in place.

As if he was following her thoughts he said:

"If you want to know, that is Indian packing, and it hides what is inside. I suggest however that you do not look at it until the last minute before you pass it over."

Paola laughed.

"I think I shall be so curious that I will be unable to resist looking at it."

"You will not be the only person who will feel like that," Hugo said.

He rose to his feet.

"Goodbye, my pretty Cousin," he said. "I am sure you will break a lot of Italian hearts in Lucca, but keep your own intact until you return to England. We have no wish to lose you to another country."

"That is the nicest compliment I have ever had," Paola said.

"You will have a great many more when you burst upon an unsuspecting world," Hugo prophesied. "But I do understand why it would be frustrating to stay in England and have to refuse every invitation which comes your way."

"I shall enjoy seeing Italy," Paola said.

"Well be careful that the goddesses depicted by the Old Masters are not jealous of you," Hugo said. "Otherwise they may take their revenge in a very unpleasant manner!"

Paola laughed again.

"Now you are trying to frighten me!" she protested. "I am sure that Italy will be a lesson in itself, which I am longing to have."

"Just avoid the very plausible *Signori*," Hugo advised, "and do not believe a word they say to you!"

"I will try not to," Paola promised.

But her eyes were twinkling.

"Thank you again, more than I can say," Hugo said. "I can tell you that getting rid of this diamond is a weight off my mind."

He walked towards the door and when he reached it he turned back and waved his hand.

"Goodbye," he said, "and may the Arch-Angels, or whoever is looking after you, take care of you until we meet again."

He was gone before Paola could think of an appropriate reply.

She leant back against the pillows and looked at the small package he had given her.

Her first impulse was to open it and see the diamond which had caused so much trouble.

Then she thought that would be a mistake.

If it was as enticing and as beautiful as
Hugo had said, she would want to keep
looking at it.

Then somebody else might see it and the
trouble would start.

'I cannot think why so much fuss is made
about jewels,' she thought. 'They may look
beautiful when they are worn, but people
are always worrying about thieves and burglars or Papa, fussing over insurance.'

Then she reminded herself that if she lost
the diamond or was robbed, it would cost
Hugo twenty thousand pounds of which he
was greatly in need.

"I must be careful . . . very . . . careful,"
she told herself.

She heard the maid open the door and
knew she was coming to call her.

Quickly she pushed the little parcel under
her pillow.

When she was up and dressed she hid it in
the handbag she always carried with her.

She thought as she did so that it was unlikely that anyone would see it there.

All the same as she went down to breakfast she felt a little guilty.

She had never had any secrets from her
parents.

She thought perhaps she really should tell her Mother what Hugo had asked her to do.

But she had given him her sacred promise, and anyway it would be unkind to worry her Mother.

This she would undoubtedly do if she told the Countess she was carrying anything so valuable.

The *Contessa* arrived later in the morning and Paola thought her charming.

She looked no more than forty-five Paola thought and had the same quiet dignified manner which was characteristic of her Mother.

"I hope you will not find it dull in Lucca," she said to Paola. "There are a lot of things to see there because very little has been changed over the years. It is, in fact, one of the most unspoilt of all our ancient cities."

"I am longing to see it," Paola said, "and I am sure I will be thrilled by everything and have a great deal to tell Mama when I return to England."

"I am trying to persuade your Mother and Father to come and stay while you are still with me," the *Contessa* said. "After all your Mother has Italian blood in her, which should be calling to her to come home."

The Countess laughed.

"I have become very Anglicised, and I

think that Paola, with her golden-red hair is really more Italian than I am."

"She will certainly be appreciated by my friends in Lucca," the *Contessa* said, "and I hope she will enjoy their company as much as I do."

"I am sure I shall," Paola said, "and thank you very, very much for having me. I am very grateful."

She knew the *Contessa* appreciated the way she spoke.

There was also a look of pride in her Mother's eyes.

All the same, when she went upstairs to her Bedroom to choose which gowns were to be packed she could not help feeling a little sad.

She did not really want to leave London where she had looked forward to everything being so exciting when she left School.

She had thought so much about the Balls she would attend.

It now seemed heart-breaking to have to miss them.

Hanging up in her wardrobe were the gowns her Mother had bought for her to wear.

They were all, Paola thought, very lovely and very becoming.

Yet it was pleasing to know that she would

be able to wear white and even pale colours in Lucca.

As she would be incognito there, no-one would think she was being disrespectful to her dead Grandmother.

She expected however that the *Contessa*'s friends, however charming they might be, would all be very much older than herself.

In fact, there might be no young men to pay her compliments, as Hugo had suggested.

It was not until she was actually in the train to Dover that she remembered she was not to use her title simply in order to avoid attracting the attention of the *Marchese.*

She had forgotten that when Hugo had asked her to carry the diamond to him.

Now she was aware that her Mother would think she was walking blindly 'into the lion's den.'

Paola puzzled over this for some time.

Finally she told herself there was no reason why she should actually see him.

All she had to do was somehow to get the diamond into his hands.

'But how can I do that?' she asked herself 'If I have to send one of the servants to his house, they will undoubtedly tell the *Contessa* what I have asked them to do.

She will think it very strange, particularly when she warned Mama that I should not meet him.'

It was something that kept recurring to her mind.

She thought of it all the time they were travelling across the Channel, through France, and finally into Italy.

It was a long journey which involved several changes of train.

But Paola found it exhilarating to see the countryside through the windows.

When they stopped at the stations she enjoyed listening to the Porters and people speaking first French, then Italian.

She had found Italian easy ever since she had been a child.

Her Grandmother, who had been very beautiful, had insisted that she should speak the language that was in her blood.

Although her Father had protested, she had been given Italian lessons almost before she had English ones.

She had of course also learnt French.

It was obligatory at School and the French Mistress had been delighted at her progress.

The *Contessa* was very impressed at how fluent she was in both those languages.

"I have never understood," she said,

"why, when the English go abroad, they merely speak louder instead of troubling to learn the language of the country they are visiting."

Paola laughed.

"I think the English find it difficult to believe that any language is more important than their own," she said. "I know the girls at School used to laugh at me because I really tried hard to be proficient at Italian and French."

"It is something they will regret as they get older," the *Contessa* prophesied. "You will find it so much easier to appreciate the ancient relics in Lucca when they are explained to you in Italian. There never seems to be the right adjective in English."

Paola laughed again before she said:

"Now, Ma'am, you are being prejudiced."

"I suppose I am," the *Contessa* said, "but I am very proud of my own country, and especially the City in which I live."

When finally they reached Lucca after a long drive which was very tiring, Paola was entranced by the City.

The *Contessa* had told her that the streets and Squares were full of Renaissance and Gothic buildings.

She had also said that the ramparts had

been built in the 16th and 17th centuries.

But Paola had not expected them to be so tall and overwhelming.

There were huge, projecting bastions, linked to one another by curtain walls, and four great gateways.

Paola had never seen anything like them before.

They made the City seem mysterious and exciting from the moment she passed through them.

The *Contessa*'s Villa, which was also old, was near the Cathedral, and had a beautiful garden.

Paola felt she wanted to explore everything immediately.

But the *Contessa* said wisely that they had had a long journey.

The first thing they should do was to rest.

"You will find it easier to sleep in a comfortable bed than a rattling train," she said.

This was true.

Paola slipped into the bed which was in an attractive room overlooking the garden.

She fell asleep and did not wake until noon the following day.

When she went down to luncheon, having missed breakfast altogether, she was very apologetic.

"Please do not apologise my dear," the

Contessa said. "It was the most sensible thing you could do. While I admit to having had a very good night's sleep, I am still feeling tired."

When luncheon was finished Paola went into the garden.

It was filled with flowers and beautifully kept.

She wandered along, thinking how attractive everything seemed in the sunshine.

Then the tolling of a Church-bell reminded her that she was near the Cathedral, which she longed to visit.

It was only a short distance away.

She had seen when she arrived how spectacular it looked with an imposing green and white marble façade.

She walked into the Villa to look for the *Contessa.*

When she reached the Drawing-Room, she heard voices.

She paused, wondering who was visiting the *Contessa* so soon after their arrival.

Then she heard a woman's voice say in Italian:

"My dear, he arrived yesterday. I thought he had forgotten our existence and would never come back to Lucca!"

"I am sure he found Florence very amusing," the *Contessa* said with a slightly

63

cynical note in her voice.

"We all know that," her visitor replied. "'I hear that the *Marchese* has been having a wild love-affair with Princess Leone who, as you know, has been acclaimed as the most beautiful woman in Florence."

"Has she come with him?" the *Contessa* asked.

"No, he is alone and it makes me wonder what has happened. Can he be bored with her, as he has been with so many other Beauties? Or do you think that Prince Gustavo, who is known to be very jealous, has thrown him out?"

The *Contessa* laughed.

"I should think that is very unlikely, but one never knows where the *Marchese* is concerned."

"No, indeed!" her friend answered. "And of course he will be looking more handsome, more exciting and more raffish than ever!"

Paola was suddenly aware that she was eavesdropping.

They were obviously talking about the *Marchese di Lucca.*

That meant he could receive the ring as soon as she could get it to him.

She had of course no idea as yet how she could do this.

But it would certainly now be much easier than if he were in Florence.

After a little pause she opened the door and entered the room.

She found there was an attractive woman sitting beside the *Contessa,* who exclaimed how delighted she was to meet her.

"Now that you are back, Marta," she said to the *Contessa,* "we must have a party. My son is returning home in a few days, and with him my nephew. I know they will be thrilled to meet Miss Forde."

"You are very kind," the *Contessa* said, "and of course we will be delighted to come to you, and for you and your family to come to us."

"We will do both," was the answer.

When she had gone, the *Contessa* said:

"My friend is a very kind person, but a terrible chatter-box. I am sure she will now rush all over Lucca, telling everybody you have arrived — a new face is always welcome here."

"What I want to do first," Paola said, "is some sight-seeing. In fact I came in from the garden to ask if we might visit the Cathedral."

"Yes, of course," the *Contessa* agreed, "and as it is very near, we just have to walk across the road. It is only right that you should see it first, as I think it is far the most impressive building in the whole City."

They put on their hats and walked across the road.

They admired first the three great doors of the West Front of the Cathedral and the enormously tall campanile.

Inside, Paola was immediately conscious of an atmosphere which seemed to her to be vibrant with faith.

She had been brought up as a Catholic because her Mother was one.

Her Grandmother had, when she married the 5th Earl, made a somewhat unusual arrangement.

It was that all their girl children should be brought up as Catholics and the boys as Protestants.

Paola always thought it very sad for her Father that she had no brothers.

Therefore she had often accompanied him to his Church, which was in the grounds of their house in the country.

But she had also attended Catholic Services with her Mother.

These took place in a small Church in a nearby village.

Immediately she entered the Cathedral, which was dedicated to St. Martin, she felt as if the whole building enveloped her with a

66

feeling of protection.

She was acutely aware of the spirituality of it.

Because she had read so much about Italy's Saints she was delighted to see to her left as she entered through the main door there was a Chapel to St. Francis of Assisi.

She bought a candle and lit it.

Then kneeling in front of the altar she sent up a special prayer to St. Francis.

She asked him to help her pass the diamond to the *Marchese* without there being any difficulty about it.

"Please, help me, St. Francis," she whispered, and felt as if he responded to her prayer.

There was far too much to see in the Cathedral on one visit.

The *Contessa* showed her the *Volto Santo,* which means, 'Holy Visage.'

It was a miraculous Crucifix, which it was said Nicodemus got possession of after Calvary.

On it he had carved a likeness of Christ.

There were a great many legends about the *Volto Santo.*

When they returned to her Villa, the *Contessa* related them to Paola.

"I tell you what I will do," Paola said. "I will write down an account of all the lovely things, like the legends you have just told me. I know Mama will enjoy hearing about them."

"In other words — you are going to write a book," the *Contessa* said with a smile.

"Why not?" Paola said. "I have often thought it is something I would love to do. But first I must travel all over the world to get material for it."

"That is certainly very ambitious," the *Contessa* laughed. "I am sure there are dozens of ancient artefacts in Lucca, each one of which could make a book on its own!"

"I will start anyway with one. But of course you must help me," Paola said.

"I will certainly try," the *Contessa* promised.

When she went up to bed that night, Paola lay thinking about the Cathedral.

She was also planning what she would write down for her Mother to read.

Suddenly she had an idea.

It came to her so forcefully that she felt it must be St. Francis who was telling her what to do.

She had been wondering how she could get the diamond to the *Marchese* without anybody being aware of it.

Also, because it would appease her conscience as regards her Mother, how she could give him the diamond without actually meeting him.

She was so excited by the idea that had come to her that she got out of bed.

Lighting a candle she sat down at the small writing-desk that stood in a corner of her Bedroom.

It took her some time to consider what she should say.

Finally she wrote in English, having made two or three attempts at what she wanted.

Then she read carefully:

"I have something that you have been promised and are expecting. If you will go to the Chapel of St. Francis in the Cathedral on Friday morning at nine o'clock, you will receive it."

Paola read it through several times to be sure it was clear enough for the *Marchese* to understand.

It must not, she knew, convey to anybody else any particular information.

She chose Friday because that was two days ahead.

She thought nine o'clock was a time when there would not be many people in the Cathedral.

69

It should not be too early for the *Marchese.*

She had noted when she visited the Cathedral that the Communion Service was at seven o'clock.

There were no Services after that until much later in the day.

"I hope I have done the right thing," she worried.

She looked again at the plain piece of paper on which she had written her message.

She folded it, put it into an envelope and addressed it to:

"MARCHESE VITTORIO DI LUCCA."

There was still the difficulty, she knew, how to have it delivered to the Villa Lucca where he lived.

She had passed it as they drove to the *Contessa*'s Villa, on the afternoon of their arrival.

Seen through large important gates the Villa looked exceedingly beautiful.

She would have loved to stop and look at it.

But they had flashed past.

All she had was an impression of white Marble, two statues on either side of the front door and two more on the floor above it.

"I will see everything in Lucca — except for that!" she had told herself.

She knew it was impossible not to be a little curious.

Not only about the Villa, which was so outstanding, but also about the man to whom it belonged.

"I must behave in a circumspect manner, as Mama would expect me to," Paola told herself.

At the same time, she was wondering how she could get the letter she had written to the *Marchese*.

She put it into her hand-bag.

The next morning the *Contessa* announced that they were going sight-seeing.

Paola felt in some inexplicable way that either her Guardian Angel or St. Francis would help her to get the note to the *Marchese*.

It was easier to walk than to drive.

They went down the narrow streets and alleys, Paola finding everything fascinating.

The old Town had some of its Roman buildings still intact.

The *Palazzo Mansi* housed fascinating pictures that Paola had read about, but never expected to see.

It was on the way back that they stopped at a shop.

It had the most delightful pottery which was one of the great arts of Tuscany.

The *Contessa* had already given an order for some new crockery, which had not yet arrived.

While she was talking to the Shop-keeper, Paola realised that the Villa Lucca was only a short distance away.

She could see the gates quite clearly.

The *Contessa* was being shown some more pottery at the back of the shop.

Moving swiftly, Paola ran as fast as she could down the street to the gates of the Villa.

She was not surprised to see that just inside, tending the grass and the flowers, were two gardeners.

Pushing open the gate which was ajar, she hurried to the nearest man.

She put the letter into his hand saying:

"Please, give this to the *Marchese*. It is very important."

The gardener, who was a young man, looked up at her and smiled.

"I will do that, Signorina," he promised.

There was a look of admiration in his eyes as he spoke.

"Thank you, thank you very much,"

Paola said hurriedly.

She went quickly back towards the shop where she had left the *Contessa.*

She only slowed down at the last moment as she reached it.

She made it appear as if she was looking round outside the shop.

The *Contessa* came out of the shop.

"Oh, there you are, Paola!" she said. "I wondered what had happened to you."

"I was thinking how fascinating this narrow street is," Paola said. "I am sure it must have seen so many people pass by from the days of the Romans. I expect it was the over-dressed but very beautiful ladies who started the silk trade here in the 14th Century."

"I see you have been mugging up on your History," the *Contessa* smiled, "and of course you must write it all down for your Mother. Do not forget that after Napoleon's Italian Campaign he bestowed the title of 'Princess of Lucca' on his Sister."

"I will certainly include that!" Paola said.

"We had better make our way home now," the *Contessa* went on. "Luncheon will be ready, and I am sure you have seen enough already this morning to write two books, let alone one!"

As Paola hurried back towards the Villa,

she could not help feeling a little guilty.

She wondered what the *Marchese* would think when he read her note.

She was half-afraid he would think it was a hoax.

Then she thought he would have had Hugo's letter by now.

Although he might think it a strange way to receive the diamond ring, she felt he would be too curious not to go to the Cathedral.

If the diamond had such a history, he would do anything to get it back into his keeping.

'What I have to do,' Paola decided as they walked back to the Villa, 'is just to place it in his hand, then vanish. There is no reason why he should thank me. He will not know who I am, or even if it was I who brought the diamond from England.'

'I really have been very clever,' she told herself as she walked into her bedroom. 'I need not be involved with the *Marchese*, which would upset Mama, and I shall have kept my word to Hugo. No-one could ask more than that!'

She smiled at herself in the mirror as she sat down at the dressing-table.

Just to make certain it was still there she took it out of her hand-bag.

Then it was impossible to resist the temptation to look at it.

She took out the little parcel that Hugo had given her.

She looked at it curiously before she went across the room to lock the door.

Slowly, because it was so exciting, she undid the coarse cotton that was wound round the linen.

Now, for the first time, she saw the diamond.

She could only gasp as she took it out of its wrapping.

It was the most beautiful, and certainly the largest diamond she had ever seen.

It was affixed to a ring, but was really too big to be worn as one.

It was heavy, and it shone and sparkled.

It seemed as if the sun coming through the window swept into the centre of it and sent out myriad lights from the diamond itself.

Gazing at it, Paola could understand why men were prepared to fight and even to die for a gem of such loveliness.

Because it glittered in the sunshine, it seemed to have a life of its own.

It was hard to credit that she had carried it all these days in her hand-bag, wrapped in a piece of linen.

She could not resist putting it on the third finger of her left hand, like an engagement ring.

She could understand that any woman being given such a gift would consider herself crowned with glory.

Then she wondered who was to be the recipient of such splendour.

Would it be the beautiful Princess about whom she had heard the *Contessa*'s friend talking?

Or was there somebody even more important in his life?

Suddenly she was afraid that somebody might knock on her door.

Hastily she wrapped up the diamond as it had been before. Hugo had told her how he had nearly lost his life in retrieving it for the *Marchese.*

She had a sudden thought that perhaps whoever received the ring would incur bad luck, and not good.

She did not want to think about that.

Quickly she put the ring back into her hand-bag.

Somehow, and she was not certain why, she did not want to look at it again.

It frightened her!

CHAPTER FOUR

Paola stepped out of her Bedroom shortly before nine o'clock.

She had been called at eight with her breakfast, but she knew the *Contessa* never woke before nine.

She had learnt too that her hostess had no wish to see anybody before she was dressed.

She had been very attractive when she was young.

Now she resented, although she did not often say so, that she was growing older.

Paola therefore knew that she was quite safe in slipping out of the Villa to go to the Cathedral.

She would be able to give the ring to the *Marchese* if he came as she had asked him to do.

She would be back in the Villa long before the *Contessa* realised she was missing.

Thinking it would be a mistake to go looking too smart, she had chosen a simple white gown.

Instead of one of her attractive hats, she decided to wear over her head a long scarf that looked like the small shawls the Italian women wore when working in the fields.

She took the ring out of her hand-bag.

She hesitated for a moment, then un-wrapped it from the handkerchief in which she had concealed it.

As she had done yesterday, she put it on the third finger of her left hand, twisting the diamond into the palm of her hand where it would not show.

It glittered and gleamed in the sunshine coming through the window as she did so.

She thought as she had done before that it seemed to have a life of its own.

She was still not certain whether it was a good or an evil one.

As she walked down the stairs she saw a maid carrying a tray containing the *Contessa*'s breakfast into her bedroom.

"I have planned it very cleverly," Paola again congratulated herself.

It was a lovely day and so far not too hot, with a slight breeze.

She went out into the sunshine.

She thought the flowers in the front of the Villa and the main street which led to the Cathedral where delightful.

There was so much for her to see in Lucca.

She almost grudged the time the *Contessa* insisted on being in the Villa and resting.

"There is no hurry, my dear," she had said to Paola yesterday. "You will be here until the end of the Summer, and once you have seen everything, perhaps you will be bored."

"I think it would be impossible to be bored in Lucca," Paola answered. "I never imagined any City could be so attractive, or have so many beautiful buildings."

"That is what I feel myself," the *Contessa* said, "and when I travel to other countries, I am always glad to come home."

Now Paola was walking alone.

She knew if she was behaving properly she would have taken a servant with her.

She therefore hurried towards the Cathedral.

There were very few people about and she was sure that no-one who noticed her would suppose from the way she was dressed that she was of any importance.

A few minutes later the Cathedral came in sight.

She thought again how beautiful it was with its arched doorways and huge campanile towering above it.

The latter was built of stones of two different colours and looked more unusual than any town Paola had ever seen before.

She entered the Cathedral and was relieved to see at a glance that there were very few people inside.

As she went towards the Chapel of St. Francis she saw there was nobody there.

Crossing herself with Holy Water, she bought a candle.

There were several candles already alight in the Chapel.

She wondered whether those who had lit them had asked a special favour of St. Francis.

Perhaps they were just venerating him for his kindness and love of birds.

Holding the candle in her left hand, she went first to where the others were burning.

She was praying as she did so that the *Marchese* would appear so that she could give him the diamond.

She could feel it cool and rather lumpy in her closed left hand.

She was coming to the end of her prayer when she became aware of a sound behind her.

She turned her head and saw a man.

He seemed to be peeping at her from behind one of the massive columns of the Nave.

It was only a quick glance, but she knew

instinctively that it was not the *Marchese.*

She wondered why the man should be staring at her.

She had her back to him again.

Yet she was conscious, and was sure it was not part of her imagination that she was being watched.

She could almost feel his vibrations touching her.

Quite suddenly she felt afraid.

There was in fact very little light in the Cathedral, but the glimpse she had had of him made her think he did not look like an Italian.

She might have been mistaken, but she was sure his skin was very much darker.

Everything that Hugo had said about there being danger in what she was doing came surging back to her.

On an impulse, because there was still no sign of the *Marchese,* she decided she must hide the ring.

She raised the candle to her lips as she had been taught to do when she had been still a small child.

Then she lit it from one of the other lighted candles.

As she did so, she slipped the ring from her left finger over the base of the candle.

Very carefully she placed it in line with

the other candles burning below the image of St. Francis.

Only as she finished hiding the ring was she aware that a different man had entered the Chapel from another direction.

He had come in by the West door of the Cathedral.

It was as if he had been looking at the High Altar before coming down the side aisle.

One glance at him told Paola that this was undoubtedly the *Marchese.*

He was tall and broad-shouldered, with dark hair swept back from a square forehead.

She had expected him to be handsome after all the things that had been said about him.

Now she knew unmistakably that he had come, as she had asked him to do, to receive the ring.

She thought immediately that she had been very stupid in hiding it where she had.

She glanced behind her again, but there was no sign of the other man.

Yet she was instinctively aware that he was still there.

On an impulse she moved away from the lighted candles, genuflected to the altar and walked to where the *Marchese* was standing.

He was looking up at the statue of St. Francis.

"You have . . . come," she said softly, "as I thought . . . you would . . . but . . ."

She opened her lips to tell him where the ring was hidden.

Then four men, moving so swiftly that she could hardly realise what was happening, surrounded them.

There was one on either side of them and two behind.

Before they spoke Paola felt something hard pressing against the small of her back.

"Unless you wish to be injured," one of the men said, "you will go where we lead you, and if you protest or make any noise you will die!"

Paola gave a gasp and she knew the *Marchese* stiffened.

Then he asked in a calm, unhurried voice:

"What is all this about?"

"You will learn that later," one of the men behind them answered. "Now move as we have told you to do — unless you want to be man-handled."

He was speaking, Paola realised, in fluent Italian.

However his pronunciation was coarse, and his voice gutteral.

As if the *Marchese* knew they were powerless to do anything but what they ordered, he followed the man who walked just ahead of him.

Because there was a man beside her and another behind, she could do nothing but follow the *Marchese.*

She could feel her heart beating frantically because she was so frightened.

She knew exactly why they were there.

She wondered if it would be best to tell them where she had hidden the ring.

They would perhaps then leave her and the *Marchese* alone.

Even as she thought of it she remembered how Hugo had almost died in obtaining it.

And specially what it meant to him if the *Marchese* received it safely.

'What . . . shall I . . . do? What . . . shall I . . . do?' she asked herself.

In the meantime she was vividly conscious of what she knew was a revolver pressing against her back.

She could not really believe that the men would shoot both her and the *Marchese* in cold blood while they were in the Cathedral.

Yet there was no-one about and if they did so, there would be plenty of time for them to escape.

'What . . . shall I . . . do?' Paola asked herself again.

She was aware that they were moving fast towards the High Altar, then behind it.

Still there was no-one to be seen.

There was only the sound of their foot-steps as they walked over the flagged floor.

She thought she could also hear the heavy breathing of the man behind her.

Now in front there was a dark doorway.

She was sure although she had never seen it before, that it led down to the crypt.

She felt it was dangerous to go below ground with these men.

But how could she and the *Marchese* fight four of them?

The crypt door was open and they went through it and started to go down the steps.

The two men in front of her each picked up a lighted lantern that had been left there.

'All this has been planned,' Paola thought.

The idea of it made her even more fright-ened than she was already.

What did they intend to do with her and the *Marchese,* and what would they say when they could not produce the ring?

There were two flights of steps leading down to the crypt.

When they reached the bottom they passed through yet another door.

It was unlocked, although a large key

was in the key-hole.

Now they were moving along what seemed to be little more than a tunnel.

The ceiling was so low that the *Marchese* was obliged to bend his head.

They passed through another unlocked door into a large cellar.

Paola could see in the light of the lanterns that it was in a state of disrepair.

There was rubble scattered over the floor, and plaster had fallen from the ceiling.

There appeared to be no other entry except by the door through which they had just come.

The two men in front came to a halt.

Then one of the men behind said:

"Now, *Signore,* tell this woman to give us the ring she has brought for you, which was stolen from me in India."

"Where it had been stolen from me!" the *Marchese* contradicted. "As you are doubtless aware, it was given to me by the *Nizam* of Hyderabad, and belongs to me personally."

"That is what you may think," the man replied sneeringly, "but as I was among the men who worked in the Mine, I consider my claim to it is greater than yours!"

He spoke in a crude and aggressive manner.

Paola, looking at him, thought that he was the most evil-looking man she had ever imagined.

He was obviously not a pure Indian.

In fact there might have been several different races in his blood.

He was much larger and stronger than the other men appeared to be and Paola mentally named him the 'Big Man'.

She knew he was evil and would have no compunction about using violence to get what he required.

He was carrying a large revolver in his hand and the man who had been behind her also carried one.

The other two men were obviously Indian, but she thought that they too had cruel expressions and shifty eyes.

"We have been brought here, very unpleasantly by force," the *Marchese* was saying. "I now suggest you let this Lady go. I have never met her before, and I very much doubt that she could give you the object you require."

"She came to the Chapel in order to deliver to you the diamond that you have been seeking these past months," the Big Man replied sharply. "Either she will now give it to me, or I will kill you both!"

Paola gave a gasp of horror, but the *Mar-*

chese said calmly:

"In which case I am quite certain the Lady will oblige you. But I would like to be quite certain that, if she does so, we can both return the way we came."

Paola was looking at him as the *Marchese* spoke and saw a flicker in his eyes.

She was almost certain that, if he did get what he wanted, he would not hesitate to kill them both to stop them informing the police what had happened.

After a moment, because it was difficult to speak, she said:

"I ... I cannot give you ... the ring ... because I do not . . . have it . . . with me."

"What do you mean — not have it with you?" the Big Man asked angrily. "You got the *Marchese* here so that you could put it into his hand."

"Y-yes ... I know," Paola said, "b-but ... I was not . . . certain if he . . . would come ... and I intended to ... arrange to make ... the handover on . . . another day."

The four men were staring at her, but she was looking only at the *Marchese*.

"I . . . I am sorry," she said to him, "I ... did not imagine that . . . anything like this ... could occur."

"Nor did I," the *Marchese* replied.

He turned towards the Big Man.

"Now you see, my good men, that we cannot oblige you, so you will have to let us go."

"Search them!" the Big Man ordered.

He almost screeched the words, which told Paola he was very angry.

The Indian who had led her was running his hands over her body.

She wanted to struggle at the indignity of it.

Then she realised that the *Marchese* was standing perfectly still as the other Indian searched him.

She therefore lifted her chin and did not move.

The Indian's hands ran over her legs and searched her shoes, in case the ring was hidden there.

The Big Man was watching.

There was no doubt of the fury in his eyes and the tightness of his lips when he realised they could not find what he wanted.

The two Indians looked at him and made a helpless gesture with their hands.

"Now you see you are mistaken, and the ring is not with us," the *Marchese* said. "I suggest you let me compensate you for your wasted journey so that you can return to where you came from."

"Do you think that will be enough for

me?" the Big Man asked angrily. "That diamond is mine, and I mean to have it!"

There was silence for a moment.

Then he said to Paola:

"Tell me where it is, so that I can take it before I set you free."

"I cannot tell you that," Paola replied. "It is in a place where you would never find it and locked away where no robber can get it out."

The Big Man suddenly turned towards her and bending so that his face was near to hers he asked furiously:

"Do you think that answer will satisfy me? I have come from one end of the world to the other to get back what is mine. You tell me where it is, and how I can obtain it, or I will keep you both here until you do."

Paola shook her head.

"It is . . . impossible . . . quite impossible . . . for you to . . . find it," she said. "If you let me . . . go back to where it is . . . then perhaps . . . we can talk . . . about it."

"While you send for the Police, I suppose!" the Big Man snarled. "Do you take me for a fool?"

There was silence for a moment, as if he was thinking.

At last he said:

"Perhaps when you are suffering from

starvation you will see sense and change your mind. No-one will ever find you here, and here you will stay until you tell me what I want to know."

Every word he spoke sounded menacing, and instinctively Paola took a step backwards.

"I warn you," the Big Man said, "if you do not tell me tomorrow what I want to know, I know of ways and means to persuade you which will be very painful!"

The words seemed to echo round the cellar.

He walked back to the door through which they had entered.

"Come on, men," he said. "We will leave them to think over what I have said."

As the men moved towards him he flung out his arm and pointed his finger at Paola.

"You think you're very clever!" he sneered. "But I shall find what we've come for and until I have the ring in my possession, you and your stuck-up partner will stay here without food and without water."

The way he spoke was so ferocious that Paola felt as if he was striking her.

Carrying one of the lanterns with him and leaving the other behind, the Big Man left the cellar.

He was followed by the three Indians.

Paola heard the key turn in the lock and their footsteps as they crossed the next cellar to slam another door.

She stood listening until she could hear them no more.

Then she turned to look at the *Marchese.*

The scarf had slipped back on her head, without even thinking what she was doing she pulled it off.

She was then aware that the *Marchese* was staring at her.

Paola looked at him.

"I . . . I am . . . sorry," she said.

"You were very brave," the *Marchese* answered. "I am quite certain that any other woman in your position would have given him the diamond."

"But . . . I am not . . . carrying it!" Paola said.

"I am well aware of that," the *Marchese* answered.

Paola realised that the Indians had been very thorough in their examination, and blushed.

"Incidentally," the *Marchese* said, "before we go any further, perhaps you should tell me who you are, and where the diamond which is causing so much trouble is hidden."

Paola thought it would be a mistake for

him to know too much about her.

"My name is Paola," she said, "and Hugo Forde asked me to bring the diamond ring to you after he had managed to get it back."

"He told me he had done so in a letter which I found waiting for me when I arrived here," the *Marchese* said, "but I suppose he was not aware how dangerous it was for you to be his messenger."

"I did not think it would be as dangerous as this," Paola announced and her voice trembled. "But . . . somebody must have . . . read the note . . . I left for you."

"That is what I have been thinking," the *Marchese* agreed. "It means there is a spy in my household and that is something I will not tolerate!"

There was a note of anger in his voice.

He still appeared calm and unruffled as he had been even when threatened by the Big Man.

"When I came to the Chapel to bring you the diamond," Paola said in a low voice, "I caught sight of the Indians, so I . . . hid the ring which I . . . had with . . . me."

"Where have you hidden it?" the *Marchese* asked.

"At the base of the candle I lit to St. Francis," Paola murmured.

Unexpectedly the *Marchese* laughed.

"How could you have thought of anything so clever? It is inconceivable that anyone would think of looking there."

"Nevertheless I am . . . sure that to-morrow I . . . shall have to . . . tell them the . . . truth." Paola faltered. "Besides, the candle will have . . . burnt down and the . . . ring will be . . . found."

"What we have to do," the *Marchese* said, "is to get out of this place, but I have no idea how."

He walked to where the lantern lay and picked it up.

Holding it as high as he could, he examined the walls on every side of the cellar.

They were in bad repair, but Paola could see that they were very strong.

She was certain they were so far below ground that, however much they called and banged on the door, no-one would hear them.

The *Marchese* walked to the far end of the cellar.

"There is another door here," he said, "but our captors obviously thought they had taken us as far as they could go."

Paola walked over to join him.

She thought despairingly that, even if this door opened into another cellar it would be the same as the one they were in now.

It would offer no chance of escaping.

The *Marchese* put the lantern on the ground and started pulling at the door.

There was no key in the lock as there had been in the other door.

It was however jammed.

It took the *Marchese,* using all his strength, somehow to pull it open.

Paola could not help thinking it was a waste of time.

It could only lead them further underground.

She felt certain that the only way out from the cellars was the way they had come.

The *Marchese* then pulled up the lantern again and passed through the doorway. Paola could only think it would be no different from the other cellars.

But because she had no wish to be alone, she followed him.

The ceiling was black and the floor was covered with stones and rubble.

There were one or two empty tins, which seemed out of place in the crypt of a Cathedral.

The *Marchese* walked on saying as if to himself:

"The only people who have been here recently have been workmen, but there appears to be some sort of fireplace."

He was looking at one side of the further wall as he spoke.

Paola followed the direction of his eyes and saw a place where a fire had been lit.

The walls around it were blackened with smoke and there was an opening in the ceiling above it.

"A chimney!" she exclaimed. "I wonder why that was built there?"

"It may come out on the outside of the building," the *Marchese* replied. "But unfortunately I doubt if I could climb up it."

He looked up at the hole in the ceiling again, and Paola did the same.

It was quite a large hole, but she could see that it was too small for the *Marchese*'s broad shoulders to squeeze through.

Paola looked at it, then looked again.

Then she said in a very small voice:

"I . . . I think . . . perhaps . . . if you will . . . help me . . . I could . . . climb up it."

The *Marchese* turned to stare at her.

"You? Do you really mean that?"

"I . . . I could . . . try," she said. "It may end abruptly, then again, it might not."

"I hate to ask you to do anything so unpleasant," the *Marchese* said after a moment's pause. "But what alternative have we?"

There was a silence, until Paola said:

"I have a feeling that . . . the Big Man will . . . come back tomorrow and . . . t-torture me until I tell him where the ring is . . . hidden."

"That is what I thought myself," the *Marchese* agreed.

Paola could see by the expression in his eyes how much the idea revolted him and she said quickly:

"Let me . . . try. It may be . . . impossible, but if I could . . . climb up . . . at least I could fetch . . . people to save you."

The *Marchese* hesitated.

"You are quite certain that you are willing to do this?"

"I am willing to . . . do anything," Paola replied, "rather than let that horrible . . . evil man take the diamond which . . . almost cost . . . Hugo his . . . life . . . not once . . . but a dozen times."

"I should never have asked him to do such a thing," the *Marchese* said angrily.

"I think," Paola said, "that it was something he enjoyed and of which now he is very proud."

She smiled before she added:

"My Father has always said that all men like a challenge, and that is certainly true of Hugo."

"And are you prepared to accept this

challenge?" the *Marchese* asked.

"What have . . . we to lose?" Paola asked. "And if I fail . . . perhaps we can find some . . . other means of . . . escape."

She thought as she spoke that that was highly improbable.

They were deep underground and locked in.

Yet there had been a fire and the smoke had obviously been able to escape up the chimney.

"Very well," the *Marchese* said as if he had been considering it in his mind, "what do you want me to do?"

"I . . . I am not . . . certain," Paola said, "but I must try to . . . prevent the soot from . . . going up my nose and . . . into my mouth."

"Yes, of course. That is sensible," the *Marchese* agreed.

He felt in his pocket and drew out a clean white linen handkerchief.

"You had better take this," he said, "and there is the shawl you had over your head."

"Yes, of course," Paola answered, "but you will have . . . to help me to . . . tie it tightly."

The *Marchese* first tied his handkerchief so that it was over her nose and covered her mouth.

Then he wrapped her long scarf over her head, bringing the ends round under her chin.

He then tied it at the back of her neck.

"That is not too tight?" he asked.

"No, not at all," Paola replied.

It was difficult to speak because her lips were covered by the handkerchief.

The *Marchese* had arranged the scarf to cover her chin also and pulled it down over her forehead.

He had in fact completely enveloped her face so that only her eyes showed.

"Try not to let the soot get into your eyes," he said. "It would sting."

He looked around.

"If there was a brush I could clean at least the lower part of the chimney."

"I will manage," Paola said bravely.

The *Marchese* bent low and looked up through the opening, holding the lantern aloft.

"It appears, as far as I can see, to be fairly wide," he said, "and there is light at the top."

Paola took off her shoes.

"I think that unless I remove my shoes I might slip on the bricks," she explained. "It will be easier without them."

The *Marchese* looked at her.

"Are you quite sure you are ready to do this?" he asked. "It is wonderfully brave of you. I cannot imagine any other woman I know behaving as magnificently as you have since those devils dragged us here."

He realised as he spoke that Paola looked shy at the compliment.

The expression in her strange green eyes with their gold flecks was very touching.

"If you save us," the *Marchese* said suddenly, "I shall be quite certain you do not really exist, but are an Angel sent by St. Francis to save us from giving the diamond to the robbers."

He knew by the expression in her eyes that Paola was moved by what he said.

Abruptly as if he felt he was wrong to let her take such a risk, he said:

"All right, if you have to do it, let us get on with it! But for God's sake be careful when you get to the top that those men do not see you."

He lifted her up as he spoke.

As Paola bent her head and went through the hole he lifted her higher and higher.

She climbed up until she was standing on his shoulders and he knew she was gripping the sides of the chimney with her hands.

Just for a moment he could hardly believe that what was happening was real.

Then he knew that Paola, whoever she might be, was the most unusual and certainly the bravest young woman he had ever met.

CHAPTER FIVE

Paola could now see clearly the light the *Marchese* had spoken about.

It was to the left of the chimney above her.

She reached up, and managed by scrambling with her feet to be no longer standing on the *Marchese*'s shoulders.

Pulling herself up higher very carefully, she drew level with the hole in the wall.

It was through this that the smoke had escaped.

She looked out of it hopefully, and then almost in despair.

It was at the very end of the Cathedral.

Below it the ground sloped away from the building and was surrounded by a massive pointed iron fence.

The ground beyond it was rocky.

Paola knew that if she tried to climb down she would be sure to slip.

Even if she was not impaled on the railings, she would at least break a leg.

It was such a disappointment that for the moment she could only just stare down below her.

She felt that in some way she had been misled.

Then she moved her right hand from the inside of the chimney to hold on to the hole.

As she did so she felt a brick give way beneath it.

Looking straight ahead she realised that while the bricks were black from smoke they were also uneven.

There appeared to be a small hole in the centre of them.

She pushed with her hands and the bricks fell down on the other side.

This was at least encouraging.

She went on pushing away at the loose bricks.

Finally the hole now facing her was the same size as the one through which the smoke had escaped.

Now she could peer through it.

She saw, although there was little light, that workmen's tools were lying about.

She felt her heart leap because this could be a way of escape.

She went on pushing out more and more bricks until it was possible to squeeze through the hole she had made.

She had some difficulty in doing so.

She felt her skirt tear and she also caught her sleeve.

But she got through the hole and into what appeared to be another cellar exactly like the one she had left.

She walked carefully over the floor which was scattered with the bricks that she had pushed down.

There were also piles of sand and pieces of plaster from the ceiling.

However she moved as quickly as she dared towards what she hoped was an entrance.

To her delight and joy the door of this cellar was open and she passed through it to another one.

She had to grope her way because now she was in complete darkness.

Then when she felt she must have walked quite a long way there was a faint light.

A door in front of her was ajar.

Now she was excited, feeling that she had escaped by a miracle and would be able to find help to save the *Marchese*.

There were steps ahead of her.

When she went up them she realised they were taking her back into the Cathedral.

She knew that she was behind the High Altar.

The staircase into the crypt had gone straight down, but this staircase was running sideways.

It was bearing, she thought, to the right side of the Cathedral.

Now she began to move very cautiously.

She was well aware how strange she must look with her face covered.

The scarf which covered her head was, like her skirt, black with soot.

What she was really afraid of was that the four men who had imprisoned them were still lingering inside the Cathedral.

If they saw her they would take her and the *Marchese* and lock them up somewhere else.

She moved on, stopping every so often to look ahead in case there was someone who would see her.

At the same time she was wondering desperately who she could get to save the *Marchese.*

It was then she saw in front of her several Confessional Boxes.

She knew that this was where she could hide until somebody in authority arrived.

Carefully, very carefully, just in case she was being watched she moved towards the first box.

There was no-one in the pews in front of it.

It was, she thought, too early for the hearing of Confessions to have started.

When she reached the Box she stood behind it for some moments.

She peeped down the aisle beyond it, to see if there were any Worshippers in the pews.

Worse still, the Indians might be lurking behind the pillars.

There was no-one.

With a sigh of relief she slipped into the Confessional Box.

As she sat down she felt almost faint from the tension from which she had been suffering.

Because it was hard to breathe she pulled the linen handkerchief from her nose.

She was aware as she did so, how dirty it was.

Because she had bent her head, soot which had covered her scarf poured on the floor.

It was then she heard someone enter the Confessional Box from the other side of the grille.

With a sudden leap of her heart she moved forward to kneel beside it.

She could hear someone moving, and after a moment she said:

"Are . . . you there . . . Father?"

She was terrified as she spoke just in case the Big Man or one of his men answered her.

Instead a deep voice replied:

"I am here, my child, and ready to hear your confession."

Paola drew in her breath.

Then, with difficulty, because she was so relieved, she said:

"Father I am in . . . terrible trouble. Some evil men have taken . . . the *Marchese di Lucca* down into . . . a cellar beyond . . . the Crypt and . . . locked him in."

She paused for breath.

Then the Priest on the other side of the grille said:

"What are you saying, my child? I do not understand."

"This is the truth, Father, and it is very important. You must send some strong men to save the *Marchese*."

"Are you telling me the truth?" the Priest asked.

"I swear on the Holy Bible itself, that what I am telling you is the truth and the *Marchese di Lucca* is in desperate danger."

"But why and from whom?" the Priest enquired.

"Some wicked men are . . . blackmailing him . . . to give them . . . something which he . . . possesses of great . . . value," Paola replied. "He must be rescued . . . at once. But the four men who have put him . . . there are . . . dangerous. Very dangerous!"

"How do you know this?" the Priest asked.

"I was seized with the *Marchese,* when we were both praying in . . . the chapel of St. Francis, and we were . . . taken down into the . . . Crypt by . . . force."

She paused for breath and then went on:

"Two of the men are . . . armed with . . . revolvers and the others may have . . . knives. You must take . . . strong and armed men with . . . you to rescue . . . the *Marchese.*"

There was silence.

Paola knew that the old Priest was wondering if he could really believe this fantastic story.

"I swear . . . to you, Father," she said, "and I am a Catholic . . . that what I am . . . telling you is . . . the truth and the . . . *Marchese* must . . . be saved."

The Priest obviously made up his mind.

"Very well, my child," he said, "I will do as you suggest and find people I can trust to go with me. You say that the *Marchese* is in the cellar beyond the Crypt."

"He is locked in . . . but I think the keys . . . which are very large . . . will have been . . . left in . . . the doors," Paola said. "If not . . . you will . . . have to . . . break them . . . down."

"And if you were with him, how did you escape?" the Priest asked.

108

He spoke as if he was still finding it hard to believe this extraordinary tale.

"I climbed up . . . a chimney . . . hoping I would be . . . able to get . . . out through the . . . opening for the smoke. But instead I broke through a wall into . . . another cellar, and from there . . . I got back up a staircase into the Cathedral. Then I saw the . . . Confessional Boxes in front . . . of me."

She thought if she could see the Priest he would be nodding his head as if he knew the route she had taken.

Then he said:

"I will go now and find men to accompany me to where you say the *Marchese* is imprisoned. Will you stay here?"

"I will stay . . . here until you . . . come for me, Father," Paola replied. "As I am . . . covered with soot . . . anyone would think I . . . looked very strange, and besides I am . . . terrified that I might . . . meet the men who took us . . . prisoner."

"I understand," the Priest said.

She heard him rise from the chair in which he was sitting.

Then he left the Confessional Box, pulling the curtain over it.

Anyone who approached would know that it was engaged.

As Paola heard his footsteps going away,

she gave a deep sigh of relief.

She had been so afraid that he would not believe her because it was such a fantastic story.

She could understand that anything like robbery and abduction in the case of someone so important as the *Marchese* would seem incredible.

Now that she was alone she undid the scarf which the *Marchese* had tied so neatly round her neck.

As she had known already it was thick with soot.

But the inside was clean, and she rubbed her face.

She felt the soot on her skin and it was not only ugly but unpleasant.

She wished she could wash her hands, but she knew she dared not leave the Confessional Box.

She must wait for the Priest's return and hope he would bring with him the *Marchese.*

Meanwhile she said a prayer of thankfulness to St. Francis.

She felt that it was he who had saved them and found them a way of escape.

She did not want to think how ghastly it would have been if she had to spend all day and all night, as the Big Man had said, without food or water.

She was quite certain the lantern would soon have burnt down and they would have been in complete darkness.

"Thank you, God! Thank you . . . St. Francis! Thank you! Thank you!" Paola said over and over again.

It seemed to her hours before there was any sign of the Priest's return.

Actually it was less than an hour before there was a sound of heavy footsteps.

She was aware that men were approaching the Confessional Boxes.

For one moment she was afraid it was not the Rescuers and the *Marchese* but the Big Man and his Indians.

They might in some secret way of their own have discovered what had happened.

Then the curtain over the Confessional was drawn aside.

The Priest to whom she had spoken asked in a deep voice:

"Are you there, my child?"

"I am here Father," Paola replied and saw behind him the *Marchese*.

Her eyes lit up.

As she stepped out of the Confessional the sunshine came through one of the stained-glass windows and touched her strange golden hair.

The *Marchese* who had only seen her in the light of the lantern knew he was right when he thought she looked like an Angel.

An Angel sent to rescue him.

He never imagined it was possible for a woman to be so beautiful and at the same time look so young and spiritual.

He could only stare at her and the men who were with him stared too.

"You are . . . safe!"

The words came from Paola's lips and were, the *Marchese* thought, like the song of a bird.

"I am safe, thanks to you," the *Marchese* answered. "Now, with the help of these gentlemen, we must get away as quickly as possible without anyone seeing us."

It was then Paola was aware of her torn, soot-stained gown.

Of her hands blackened from her climb up the chimney, and her bare toes peeping through her torn stockings.

She saw that the men surrounding the *Marchese* and the Priest were looking at her in astonishment.

Then the *Marchese* took charge.

He turned to a tall man who, like the others, was wearing a black cassock and carried over his arm a white surplice.

"Give me your surplice," he said.

It was an order and the man handed it to him quickly.

The *Marchese* took it and slipped it over Paola's head.

It covered her dirty, torn dress.

Then without saying anything he lifted her up in his arms.

"Now, if you gentlemen will go ahead, to see I am not molested," he said, "my carriage will be waiting outside the West Door."

The men, and they were a mixed collection of young Priests, Vergers and Choirmen, obediently walked ahead.

It was then Paola whispered, so that only the *Marchese* could hear:

"The candle!"

He nodded and smiled down at her, then said to the Priest:

"We have something, Father, to collect from the Chapel of St. Francis, and I think he too must be thanked that we have been rescued."

The men were walking ahead and heard what he said.

They moved across from behind the High Altar towards the narrow aisle which led to the Chapel of St. Francis.

When they reached it, without saying anything the *Marchese* carried Paola to where the candles were burning.

She felt that a million years had passed since she was last there.

It was therefore quite a surprise to see how little of her candle had burned away.

Quickly because she was sure the *Marchese* would not wish the men to know what had happened, she lifted the candle up.

She took the ring from beneath it, and then replaced it.

As if he understood what she wanted, the *Marchese* stood for a moment looking up at the Statue of St. Francis.

Then as he saw Paola's face raised too, he knew that she was praying.

Without speaking he turned back to where the men were waiting and again they led the way towards the West Door.

One of them, while they were in the Chapel, had gone to summon the *Marchese*'s carriage, and now it was directly outside.

There were only a few steps to take before the *Marchese* had deposited Paola inside.

Then he turned back and held out his hand to the Priest.

"I am deeply grateful Father, that you have saved me," he said. "I will be sending a Thank-Offering, to the Archbishop and telling him how splendidly every man here behaved in such an unexpected emergency."

He saw the pleasure in the men's eyes and shook the Priest by the hand.

They all bowed as the *Marchese* stepped into the carriage.

The horses moved off and as they did so Paola said:

"Please will you take me to where I am staying?"

Even as she spoke she wondered how she could possibly explain to the *Contessa* why she was being brought back by the *Marchese di Lucca*.

"I think it would be a mistake for you to go anywhere except to my Villa," the *Marchese* said.

Paola stared at him.

"I . . . cannot do . . . that."

"Why not?" he asked.

"Because I am staying with . . . a friend who would be very upset . . . at my . . . disappearance. I am . . . trying to think how I can . . . explain to her what has . . . happened."

As she spoke she remembered that she was still holding the diamond, which had caused so much trouble, in her left hand.

She held it out to the *Marchese* saying:

"Take it! I am sure it is unlucky and I

115

hope never, never to see it again!"

The *Marchese* took it from her and said:

"I have been wondering, not how I can explain away the ring, but how I can ever thank you for your bravery and for saving me, as you have done, from the humiliation and horror that was intended for us."

"I am sure . . . it was . . . St. Francis who . . . helped me," Paola said.

"I told you before you went up the chimney that you were an Angel," the *Marchese* said, "and now I am quite certain you are not really here and that at any moment you will fly back to the Heaven from which you have come."

Paola gave a little laugh.

"I am very . . . flattered that you should . . . say that, but at . . . the moment I am not seeking . . . Heaven, but . . . a bath!"

"That is waiting for you at my Villa!"

"No, please!" Paola pleaded. "You must understand. I am staying with . . . someone who must . . . not know what has occurred. So please will . . . you take me . . . to her Villa? It is not very . . . far away."

"Who are you staying with?" the *Marchese* asked.

For a moment Paola hesitated, then she knew it was something he was certain to learn sooner or later.

"The *Contessa* Raulo," she answered.

"Of course I know her," the *Marchese* replied, "and she will understand, as you must, that it would be very dangerous for you to be anywhere where you were not guarded, as I intend to be, by the Police and my own employees."

Paola stared at him and then she said:

"You do . . . not imagine . . . that they . . ."

". . . might try to kidnap you again," the *Marchese* said. "Why not? They are well aware that we have the diamond which they have come all the way from the East to obtain. I am quite certain they will not give up the chase easily."

Paola clasped her hands together.

"What . . . you are . . . saying is . . . frightening!"

"Of course it is," the *Marchese* replied, "and that is why I am taking you to my Villa, and why I am sending for the *Contessa* and will explain to her what has occurred."

Paola drew in her breath.

"Oh, please," she said, "you must not tell her that I brought the ring over from England. I did it to help Hugo Forde, but he made me swear I would not tell anyone else what I was doing. So the *Contessa* would be very shocked to think I have been in any way deceitful."

The *Marchese* thought for a moment and then he said:

"What we will say is quite easy! You were praying in the Chapel of St. Francis, and when the men who were pursuing me took me prisoner they took you too, so that you could not report it and give evidence against them."

"Thank you," Paola said, "but I still think the *Contessa* would think it very strange if I do not go back to her Villa."

"Leave that to me," the *Marchese* said. "When I tell her how brave you have been in saving us both from a dangerous situation, I think it is unlikely that she will ask many awkward questions."

Paola felt he was being optimistic.

Yet he obviously and reasonably had no intention of taking her to the *Contessa*'s Villa.

There was therefore nothing she could do.

They arrived at the beautiful Villa Lucca which she had only seen through the gates.

It was even lovelier than she had thought it to be.

Because the *Marchese* thought it was embarrassing for her to have to walk with her bare toes protruding through her stockings he carried her from the carriage into the

Villa and straight up the stairs.

A servant ran ahead to open a Bedroom door.

Paola found herself in one of the most beautiful rooms she had ever imagined.

It was not only exquisitely furnished: the carved and gilded bed might have stepped out of a Fairy Story.

But she was aware also of the pictures on the walls.

They were what she might have expected to find in the Galleries in Florence.

The porcelain on the mantelpiece was priceless.

The *Marchese* set her down by the fire-place.

"I suggest," he said, "as I value my carpets that you keep still until they can put a cloth on the floor on which the soot can fall while you undress."

There was a twinkle in his eyes as he added:

"I will ask the *Contessa* to bring your clothes with her and I am sending for her immediately."

Before Paola could think of anything to say, he had gone.

Two maids came hurrying in.

They helped her to undress, as the *Marchese* had suggested, on a cloth which kept

119

the soot off his precious carpet.

Then the maids brought in a bath.

The water was scented with rose petals which washed away the last remnants and smell of soot.

Paola was sitting, draped in a towelling dressing-gown which was far too big for her, when the door opened and the *Contessa* came in.

"My dear child!" she exclaimed as she walked towards Paola, "I have been worried sick not knowing what had happened to you or why you were no longer in the Villa."

"I am so sorry," Paola answered, "but I thought I would have plenty of time to go to the Cathedral to say a Prayer and then all this happened."

The *Contessa* looked round to make sure that the maids had left the room.

"The *Marchese* has told me the whole story," she said. "I am afraid your Father and Mother would be horrified, as I am, at your staying here as his guest, but he tells me it would be very dangerous for you to be with me unguarded."

Paola did not speak because she could not think of anything to say.

The *Contessa* went on:

"The *Marchese* has been most kind in asking me to stay here too, to chaperon you, and there is really nothing else we can do. At the same time, you must remember that your Father and Mother did not want you to meet him."

The *Contessa* had lowered her voice as she spoke.

Now she glanced over her shoulder before she went on:

"To make quite certain that you are in no danger from the *Marchese,* I have told him that I have brought you from England to help me with the many things I have to do."

Paola looked at her questioningly.

The *Contessa* continued as if she was feeling for words:

"I think you are aware that the *Marchese* has a very bad reputation with women, but he has always boasted he has never made love to a woman who was not as blue-blooded as himself and therefore . . ."

The *Contessa* paused a moment before she said in an even lower voice:

"As I implied you were a sort of secretary to me, I think, my dear, that will prevent us from having any anxiety about anything else."

For a moment Paola did not understand what she was saying. Then she blushed.

"I am sure the *Marchese* has not thought of me in any way like that," she said quickly.

"After all, we were fighting to save our lives!"

"Of course, of course," the Contessa agreed, "but you are very pretty, Paola, and his reputation is so bad. But now I am quite certain that you are safe."

There was nothing Paola could say.

She only thought that the whole situation was very strange.

When they were fighting to save their lives she had not thought of the *Marchese* as an attractive man.

He had merely been someone who with her was in danger from evil and unscrupulous men.

She was quite certain that he had thought of her in no other way.

"There is no need to worry Mama or Papa by saying where I am," she said aloud. "I expect, as the *Marchese* is sending for the Police, these terrible men will soon be behind bars."

"It cannot be too soon as far as I am concerned," the *Contessa* said. "Then we can go home and go on with what we were doing before all this happened."

She spoke rather sharply as if the whole situation was very annoying.

At the same time she was looking round the room with interest.

Paola was sure she was taking in the beauty of it, and the high quality of the pictures and the porcelain.

The *Contessa* rose to her feet.

"I believe the maids are unpacking your clothes in another room," she said. "I think you should get dressed and then we can go downstairs and find out what the *Marchese* is doing to catch these villains."

She made a gesture with her hands, and said:

"I simply cannot believe all this has happened in Lucca. There is so very little crime here, and I am quite certain no-one will believe the story of the *Marchese*'s diamond when they hear about it."

The *Contessa* suddenly stopped.

"Now I think about it," she said, "it is very strange that the robbers expected to find it on the *Marchese*. Where was it? Where had he put it? Surely he would not take anything so valuable with him to Church."

"I think they just . . . expected him to . . . tell them where it . . . was," Paola said quickly, "and as he would not do that, they locked us both up until they could force him to tell them."

"Oh, yes, I see," the *Contessa* said. "And now that they have come all this way, they will not wish to return to India without it."

"I am sure . . . they will . . . try again,"
Paola said, "unless they are caught and arrested."

She tried to speak impersonally, but her
voice trembled.

She knew that she was very frightened.

They had not yet escaped from the Big
Man and the Indians who obeyed his
orders.

CHAPTER SIX

Paola went down to dinner in one of the simplest gowns she had brought to Lucca with her.

She would have liked to wear one of the pretty new gowns her Mother had bought for her, but she thought it would be a mistake.

The chandeliers had now been lit and glittered from the ceilings like stars.

When Paola saw the *Marchese* in his evening-clothes she thought that no man could look more handsome and, to be truthful, more raffish.

The Dining-Room as they found when they went into dinner, was very grand and impressive.

The candle-lit table, decorated with gold ornaments and orchids, made Paola's eyes shine.

'This is just the way,' she thought, 'that Aristocrats should live.'

And who could look more Aristocratic than the *Marchese* sitting in a high-backed chair on which was carved his coat-of-arms.

The *Contessa* was on his right and Paola on his left.

He obviously put himself out to make the evening pleasant for them.

He told them stories of his travels all over the world.

These included the tale of how he had saved the life of the *Nizam* of Hyderabad.

He made it sound amusing.

Paola however was sure that it had been a very dangerous episode.

Not only was the *Nizam* lucky to be alive, but so was the *Marchese.*

Every course brought to the table was more delicious than the last.

Yet it was difficult to think of food when Paola was listening to the *Marchese* and laughing at almost everything he said.

When the *Contessa* led the way into the Drawing-Room, the *Marchese,* in French fashion, came with them.

"Now," he said, "I want to show you some of my treasures and especially my collection of snuff-boxes."

The *Contessa* was entranced and so was Paola.

The *Marchese* had found a great number of the boxes in Russia.

Many were ornamented with precious stones with exquisitely painted miniatures of Royalty on the lid of each box.

"I really feel this house should be opened

as a museum," the *Contessa* said. "It is somehow unfair that so few people can see the marvellous things you have here."

"I see them, and my friends see them," the *Marchese* replied, "and that I assure you is quite enough."

"You are a very lucky man," the *Contessa* said, "but of course you must always be careful of burglars."

What she said made Paola think once more of the Big Man and his Indians.

She had almost forgotten them in the delight of listening to the *Marchese* at dinner.

He saw the fear in her eyes and said:

"Do not worry! We are well protected at the moment and will be until those miscreants are arrested and sent to prison. We have a number of specially chosen policemen at both the back and the front of the Villa. I can assure you ladies that you can sleep peacefully without worrying until the morning comes."

He was addressing them in the plural but he was looking at Paola.

He was thinking it was impossible for any young woman to look so lovely.

Or, and this was strange, so different from anyone else he had seen before.

Being a connoisseur, he was trying to explain to himself the difference between

Paola and the other women whom he had admired.

There had been a great number of them and of many different nationalities.

It was not, he decided finally, her outward looks, but what came from within.

He could almost feel her vibrations touching his.

Because he was looking at her in a strange way Paola blushed and felt shy.

As she looked away from him the *Marchese* said:

"I feel as this is your first visit to Lucca, I should give a Ball for you, or at least arrange some festivity which would introduce you to the more attractive of our citizens."

For a moment Paola's face was radiant.

Then she remembered that secretly she was in mourning.

"No! No!" she said quickly. "I am quite happy as I am. There is so much to see in Lucca, I am sure I shall only have explored half the city before it is time to go home."

"When will that be?" the *Marchese* asked.

"Not for several months," the *Contessa* interrupted. "Paola is right. There is a great deal for her to learn in Lucca besides all I want her to do for me."

"You are puzzling," the *Marchese* said.

"I cannot understand why anyone so young and beautiful should refuse to be given a Ball."

Paola thought he was being too perceptive and she said:

"It is something I would love some time, but not just at once. I have so many other things to do first."

"And what are they?" the *Marchese* asked.

"To see Lucca and its treasures," Paola replied.

"That is exactly what I am offering you," he answered. "Tomorrow you shall see my Picture Gallery of which I am very proud."

Paola clasped her hands together.

"I should love to see that, and I have already noticed the pictures here in the Drawing-Room which are magnificent. I want to learn who painted them and why."

"That is something I shall enjoy telling you," the *Marchese* said.

The *Contessa* felt the conversation was becoming too intimate.

It was a mistake for Paola to talk to her host more than was absolutely necessary.

She rose to her feet.

"I know it is early to go to bed," she said, "but I think after the terrible experience Paola has been through today she should have a good night's rest."

"Yes, of course," the *Marchese* said. "I am selfish in wanting to keep her here."

There was something in the way he said it which gave Paola a strange feeling.

She was sure he was only being polite.

But at the same time if he did want it, she would have liked to stay with him.

The *Contessa* however walked towards the door.

The *Marchese* opened it for her and when she said 'Goodnight' he bent over her hand.

"Thank you for a delicious dinner and your hospitality," the *Contessa* said. "Paola and I are very grateful to you."

"Thank . . . you! Thank you . . . very much," Paola said.

She held out her hand and the *Marchese* took it in both his.

"I have not yet had the chance," he said, "to thank you properly for what you have done. I can only say you were utterly and completely magnificent."

He was speaking in a low voice.

The *Contessa* by this time was crossing the hall to the Staircase.

"I am . . . so very . . . very glad . . . we are . . . saved," Paola murmured.

"I will tell you how glad I am another

time," the *Marchese* said.

He was still holding her hand in both of his and now he said, almost as if he was speaking to himself:

"You are very lovely. So lovely that I am half afraid that when tomorrow comes you will have flown up into the sky."

"I shall ... still be ... here," Paola smiled.

She wanted to take her hand away as she spoke, but the *Marchese* did not let it go.

Instead he held it even tighter in his and they looked into each other's eyes.

It seemed to Paola as if the whole world faded away and she could only see the *Marchese.*

Then as they stood without moving, the *Contessa* said sharply:

"Paola!"

It was a cry which made Paola feel as if she had fallen back onto the earth.

She took her hand from the *Marchese*'s and ran to the foot of the stairs where the *Contessa* was waiting.

As they started to climb she looked back.

The *Marchese* was not watching them go.

The Drawing-Room door was open but he had disappeared.

She felt suddenly as if she had lost him.

When they reached Paola's Bedroom the

Contessa came in and kissed her 'good-night.'

"Sleep well, dear child," she said. "Tomorrow I will speak to the Chief of Police to see if we can be guarded at home in my Villa. I think it is a mistake to stay here too long!"

"I . . . I think . . . the *Marchese* . . . likes . . . having . . . us!" Paola said hesitatingly.

The *Contessa* gave a little laugh.

"He makes every woman he meets feel indispensable to him. You must, my dear, not be so stupid as to believe him."

She left the Bedroom as she spoke.

A maid came in to help Paola undress.

When she was in bed Paola found herself thinking of the *Marchese*.

How amusing he had been at dinner and how he had held her hand just now in the Drawing-Room.

He had given her a strange feeling she had not known before.

"I expect every woman feels that when she is with him," she told herself.

But somehow she was looking again into his dark eyes and everything else was slipping away.

Paola must have been asleep for nearly two hours.

She was dreaming of the treasures she had seen downstairs and thought the *Marchese* was describing them to her.

Then suddenly with a start she realised that someone was putting something over her mouth.

For a moment she could not realise what was happening.

Then she was aware that a gag had been tied tightly behind her head.

At the same time her ankles were being bound together with a rope.

She tried to struggle and scream but it was impossible.

Almost before she was conscious enough to realise exactly what was happening, she was bundled in a blanket.

Someone was lifting her out of the bed.

She knew with a feeling of terror who it must be.

Again she tried to scream and struggle.

The arms that held her were like a vise and the gag over her mouth prevented her from making the slightest sound.

Then her head was covered with another blanket.

She was being carried across the room and to her horror was pushed out through the window.

Strong ropes had been wrapped round

her body, her neck and her feet.

She felt herself being let down very slowly and silently from the first-floor, on which she was sleeping to the ground.

There were hands to remove the rope and two men carried her swiftly away from the Villa.

By now she realised she was being kidnapped and once again she was the prisoner of the Big Man and the Indians.

She was so frightened it was hard to think.

What was even more frightening was the complete silence in which everything was done.

It was almost as if the men around her were invisible.

She could hardly even hear them move, and it was only because they were carrying her that she was aware that they were actually there.

She wondered where they would take her.

It was unlikely that it would be back to the Cathedral.

They would, she feared, have some hiding-place where no-one could find her.

Perhaps they intended to kill her!

The idea was terrifying. But she made a superhuman effort to keep her head and try to work out where they were going.

She thought, although she was not sure,

that they were moving amongst trees in the garden.

Then they went through a gate of some sort, and now she was lifted into a carriage.

The back seat on which she was laid down was hard.

She was sure there were two men in the carriage with her.

In which case the other two must have climbed upon the box with the driver.

As they drove off quite swiftly, she could hear it was drawn by only one horse.

She tried to puzzle out which direction they were taking.

She had the idea that she had been taken out of the garden by a small gate which faced in the same direction as the Great Gate.

The one through which she had run to give the gardener the note to the *Marchese.*

Now they were turning away and she was sure they were going East and not West towards the Cathedral.

If this was so, her heart sank.

She had learnt from the *Contessa* that the East side of the City was the poorest part.

All the grand Villas like hers and the *Marchese*'s were in the West.

Paola thought she might be hidden in some small cottage or in the cellar of an unknown house.

It could take weeks, if not months to search for her.

In fact it would be quite impossible for the *Marchese* to find her.

Because she was so frightened she began to pray.

Praying fervently to God and St. Francis and every other Saint she loved to help her.

"Help me! Help me!" she said over and over again.

Somehow she found herself praying to the *Marchese* also.

He would learn that her bed was empty the following morning and would perhaps believe that his prophecy had come true.

She had flown back into the sky!

"Save me! Save . . . me!"

The words repeated and repeated themselves to the rumble of the wheels as they drove over cobbled streets.

She was quite sure these were part of the very poorest part of the City.

At last the carriage came to a stop.

Paola was lifted out by the same invisible hands and carried into a building.

The floor was rough and the men walked a long way and up some stairs before they finally set her down.

Now she was sitting on a chair.

The blanket which covered her head was pulled away.

As she expected, the first face she saw was that of the Big Man.

Ugly and evil, he was even more revolting than when she had last seen him in the Cathedral.

"We meet again!" he said, in his common rough voice. "You see I have my own source of information in the Villa Lucca! This time, you'll not escape."

As he spoke Paola looked up at him, then knew where she was.

She was in the ramparts!

There was no mistaking the heavily arched ceiling, the great thick walls of rough stone, undecorated and ominous in their strength.

One of the Indians at a signal from the Big Man undid the gag which had covered Paola's mouth.

It had been very tight and painful.

She was glad when the rope which was round her body was released and she could raise her fingers to her lips.

She was then aware that she was sitting on a hard chair and beside her was a rough wooden table.

At another signal from the Big Man one of the Indians brought a blotter.

On it there was a piece of white writing-paper, and an ink-pot in which stood a quill pen.

Paola looked at it and the Big Man said:

"Now you're going to write what I tell you."

As he spoke he drew a long sharp knife from his pocket.

As Paola winced away from him in terror, he bent forward and seized a piece of her hair which was falling over her shoulders.

He hacked it away with his knife and threw it down on the table.

"What are . . . you . . . doing?" Paola cried. "Why are . . . you cutting . . . my hair?"

She had a terrified feeling he was going to cut it all off.

The Big Man merely said:

"Write what I tell you!"

Then, almost as if she was being inspired by St. Francis himself, Paola had an idea.

If she was to write to the *Marchese* as she was sure the Big Man intended, asking him to exchange her for the ring, she must try to tell him where she was.

It would be very difficult.

But she felt he would look in her letter for some word which would give him the clue he needed.

With an effort, because her mouth was so

138

dry it was hard to speak, she said:

"If you . . . want me to . . . write I . . . cannot write what . . . you tell me . . . in Italian."

"Why not?" the Big Man asked sharply.

"Because I am . . . English. Although I can . . . speak a . . . little Italian I can . . . only write in my . . . own language."

The Big Man frowned.

She could see this was an obstacle he had not expected.

Then he said:

"Write in English, but Ali can understand English and if you try to betray to the *Marchese* where you are I will kill you."

Paola gave a little shiver.

Then bravely because she knew this was her only chance she said:

"You tell me . . . what to . . . say and I will . . . write it in . . . English."

There was a little pause and she knew the Big Man disliked giving in to her.

At the same time he had no alternative.

"Write this!" he said abruptly.

"I'm a prisoner and this is my hair."

Paola wrote down in English what he had said.

He looked over her shoulder as if he

was trying to read it.

Then he went on:

"If you do not give us the ring by nine o'clock tomorrow morning, my capturers will send you for every day you make them wait one of my fingers and then one of my toes."

Paola gave a little shriek.

"You cannot . . . mean that! How can you . . . be . . . so cruel, so . . . wicked?"

"You write what I tell you!" the Big Man said. "Or I'll send him the tip o' your nose!"

Trembling at the way he spoke Paola wrote what he had said.

"Put the ring," the Big Man went on, *"outside the garden-gate, but if anyone follows or arrests the man who is sent for it, I'll die, and you'll never see me again."*

His gutteral voice ceased and Paola whispered: "You . . . cannot mean . . . this!"

"I mean it!" the Big Man said. "Now sign your name."

Paola lifted her pen again and then she wrote:

"I shall be watching every minute

passing until the sun rises, praying that you will save me.

Paola."

"What have you said that I have not told you to say?" the Big Man asked angrily.

Paola translated it for him into Italian.

She thought he might protest but instead with an unpleasant smirk he said quickly:

"That should bring me the ring, before I cut off your finger."

Although she did not want to show how frightened she was, Paola took her hands off the table and pressed them against her body.

The Big Man made her read what she had written.

Then he put the letter into an envelope with Paola's hair.

He gave it to one of the Indians with a number of instructions as to where he must leave it.

Paola did not listen.

She was only praying the *Marchese* would get it before the Big Man cut off her finger.

She felt this was some horrible nightmare from which she could not awaken.

She looked at the strength of the walls.

The great rounded bastions outside had

141

resisted enemy after enemy.

She could not think of any way in which the *Marchese* could break in and save her.

She could only go on praying as she had said in the letter she would.

Now she was asking God and St. Francis to make the *Marchese* understand she was in a Watch-Tower and it was on the East side of the City.

"Make him understand God," she prayed, "and let him save me before I lose my finger."

She felt her whole body shivering at the thought of the agony of it.

Then she knew that only by a miracle could anyone rescue her from the vast Mediaeval Bastions which encircled Lucca.

The *Marchese* was fast asleep when Ugo came into his room.

He was carrying a candle which he set down by the bed.

Then he said in a low but clear voice:

"Wake, master — wake!"

The *Marchese* opened his eyes.

For a moment he thought it must be morning.

Then he realised the room was dark.

"What is it? What has happened?" he asked.

In answer Ugo held out an envelope.

"Where did this come from?" the *Marchese* asked as he sat up in bed.

"A man threw it over the gates at the policeman guarding them," Ugo replied. "He had come swiftly out of the darkness and had gone before they could see him."

The *Marchese* opened the envelope.

As he pulled out the paper, a lock of Paola's golden hair fell on to the sheet.

He stared at it, then read what was written.

When he had done so, he sprang out of bed, picking up his robe which lay over a chair.

He opened the door and carrying a candle, ran down the corridor.

He burst into Paola's Bedroom.

By the light of his candle he saw at one glance what had happened.

The empty bed from which two blankets had been removed and the wide open window.

He looked outside and saw two policemen lying on the ground apparently unconscious or dead.

Other policemen were bending over them.

He went back to his own room and started to dress.

While he did so, he was reading again and again the letter Paola had sent him.

He was sure she had put somewhere in it an indication of where she was.

Then almost as if he could feel her speaking to him, he knew that she was praying that he would understand and he did.

It was four o'clock in the morning.

He ran down the stairs to find the policeman who was in charge of the others waiting for him.

"What has happened? How could this have occurred?" the *Marchese* asked sharply.

"I can only apologise, *Signore Marchese,*" the policeman replied, "but when you told us there were Indians who were threatening you, we did not understand they were Thuggees."

"Thuggees!" the *Marchese* exclaimed.

He knew only too well that these were the most dangerous men in India.

They had been almost exterminated in the past twenty-five years.

Yet their method of strangling a man so quickly and so efficiently that he was dead before he could struggle had been an art known to a number of much feared tribes.

"Both the policemen at the back of the

Villa have been strangled," the Chief Policeman was saying.

"No-one saw what happened or how the men managed to reach them without being observed."

The *Marchese* knew this was all part of Thuggee.

There was no point in explaining it to an Italian Policeman.

He merely said:

"I want your most reliable and experienced men here as quickly as possible, all of them armed. And I want to know which of the Ramparts on the East of the City are being repaired."

"There is only one, *Signore,*" the Policeman told him.

"Then hurry and get your men," the *Marchese* said sharply.

He glanced up at the sky as he spoke.

He was afraid that the evening stars would already have gone and the first rays of the sun were appearing.

As he did so, he was quite sure he could hear Paola calling him.

He felt as if his whole body responded in answer to her prayer.

"I will save you! I swear I will save you!"

He was not certain if he said the words aloud or in his heart.

145

But he had a strange feeling that they would reach her.

After the man had been sent away with the letter, the Big Man and the other Indians moved out of the room where Paola was.

She could hear them talking next door.

The walls however were so thick that she could not distinguish what they were saying.

They had left her without undoing the ropes round her ankles, but she now managed with some difficulty to untie them.

They had been very tight and hurt her.

The men had left one candle behind.

Now she could see more clearly what sort of place it was in which she was imprisoned.

The *Contessa* had told her how thick the walls of the ramparts were.

She also said how unusual it was to find intact mediaeval Ramparts like those which encircled Lucca.

"There are four miles of them," she had said proudly, "and everyone in the City is prepared to subscribe to keep them in good repair."

Paola peeped through the door the men had left open behind them.

She could see that this part of the rampart was definitely in need of repair.

Bricks had fallen onto the floor.

There were holes in the floor itself, and at one place near the end of the passage she could see the ceiling had fallen in.

She guessed that this was why the Big Man and his Indians had been able to find a way into the ramparts.

It made a very effective prison.

She was quite sure that no-one would think of looking for her in such an unlikely place.

She had understood that the ramparts were kept closed and locked except when they were opened for visitors.

Would the *Marchese* understand or guess from what she had written that she was in what the English would call a Watch-Tower?

There was a very different word for it in Italian.

Would he understand from her writing, 'until the sun rises,' that the Watch-Tower in which she was held was on the East side of the City?

It had been too risky to make it any clearer.

Surely the *Marchese* who was so astute and had travelled so much, would understand what she was trying to tell him.

She went back and sat down in the chair.

It was the only piece of furniture in the room except the table.

Even as she did so the Big Man came from the next room.

"I'm locking you in," he said, "so you'll not be able to escape. If you try I'll kill you. Just you stay put and hope the ring comes, or you'll lose the first finger of your left hand."

He was deliberately provoking her.

Although she was so terrified Paola managed to raise her chin.

"I believe God will help me," she said quietly, "just as He helped me escape from the last place you imprisoned us."

"I'll take care you don't do that again," the Big Man said in an ugly voice, "but of course that *Marchese* you fancy may decide he has plenty of other women besides you!"

He almost spat the last words at her, and Paola thought it would be undignified to answer him.

She turned her face away and the Big Man said in a sudden fury:

"I'll have that ring back from him, if I've to kill him for it. That's what I'll do, sooner or later, you mark my words!"

He turned away as he spoke and slammed the door behind him.

It was very heavy.

When Paola heard the key turn in the lock she knew she was imprisoned in a place from which there could be no escape.

She had the feeling, after what the Big Man had said, that even if he got the ring back he would take his revenge on the *Marchese* and on her.

'If I have to die,' Paola thought, 'I hope he is with me. I should be even more frightened alone.'

As she thought of it she wanted to scream and go on screaming.

She was shut in and the thickness of the walls made it impossible for anyone to break out.

'I do . . . not want . . . to die,' she was thinking. 'There is so much in . . . the world I want . . . to see. There is so much I want . . . to do.'

The *Marchese* had promised to show her his treasures.

She knew his Picture Gallery would be entrancing.

She felt again that strange feeling she had felt when he had held her hand in both his.

When they looked into each other's eyes.

He was so handsome.

Yet as the Big Man had said, he had so many women, why should he worry about her?

Perhaps he would just ignore the threatening letter and let her die.

He would have every excuse to say that he could not find her.

Now her whole body was reaching out towards him.

She was pleading with him and praying for him to come to her.

She felt as if her prayers were like doves flying out from her breast towards him.

They would tell him where she was.

"Come to . . . me! Save . . . me! Save . . . me!" she begged.

She felt she could see his eyes looking into hers.

She could feel his hands and the closeness of his body.

"Come to . . . me! Please . . . come to . . . me!"

It was a prayer which came not only from her heart, but from her soul.

She had a conviction that he must hear her.

CHAPTER SEVEN

Paola opened her eyes.

She thought that she had been praying for so long that she must have dozed off.

She was still sitting on the chair beside the deal table.

The Big Man had left on it the ink she had used for the letter to the *Marchese* and also a lantern.

The latter had burnt out.

Then Paola realised that there was some light in the room.

She saw what she had not noticed before.

That in the wall at the far end there was an arrow-slit aperture.

It had been dark outside when she had been brought here, and it had never struck her for a moment that there was a window, or any way of looking out from the enormously thick wall that enclosed her.

Now she realised there was a faint light coming through an arrow-slit and it was dawn.

It was then, as if someone had struck her a blow, she realised that the sun was rising in the east and the *Marchese* had not come to save her!

He could not have understood, or perhaps he was no longer interested.

She could not believe the latter was the truth.

At the same time, the mere thought of it was like a knife turning in her heart.

Stiffly pulling the blanket around her, she walked towards the arrow-slit.

She discovered if she stood on tip-toe she could peep through it.

The glass with which it had been filled in later was thick and very dirty.

But Paola was right in thinking that the dawn was breaking.

There was only a faint twinkle of the stars overhead, and the light was rising into the sky.

She stood trying to look out.

At the same time she felt a dull despair that the *Marchese* had not understood.

She could hardly believe that the Big Man would really cut off her finger.

But she could see the gap in her hair which hung over her shoulders.

That was where he had cut away a piece over four inches long.

'Nothing can save me now,' she thought, as the light grew brighter.

Then there was gold in the sky and a few

moments later the first tentative fingers of the sun.

She felt as if she was watching the last flicker of her own life.

When the Big Man did come, he would not only cut off her finger, but perhaps kill her!

It was at that moment she heard his voice, gruff and noisy.

He was saying something to the men with whom he had spent the night in the adjacent room.

His voice was getting louder and she found it impossible to breathe.

She turned round from the arrow-slit as she heard him put the key in the lock.

The door swung open.

As he came in, she could see he was carrying in his right hand the long sharp knife with which he had cut off her hair.

He stood there looking at her, she thought, with an evil enjoyment.

She was his victim, and she could not escape.

Then he walked forwards holding up his knife so that the light from the sun glittered on it. Paola screamed.

Even as she did so there was a resounding report which seemed to echo and re-echo round the room.

The Big Man toppled forward with a crash.

Behind him in the doorway was the *Marchese.*

He was there, seeming to fill the whole place with his presence, with a smoking revolver in his hand.

Paola gave another cry which came from her very heart.

She dropped the blanket she was holding round her and ran just in her nightgown towards the *Marchese.*

She flung herself against him.

As his arms went round her she cried:

"You . . . have . . . come! You . . . have . . . come! You . . . understood! I have been . . . so frightened! So very . . . frightened!"

"I knew you must be," the *Marchese* said, "but I had to wait for that Devil to unlock the door."

As he was speaking he was looking down at her.

At her eyes looking up into his, with the tears running down her cheeks.

He thought that it was impossible for any woman to look so lovely but at the same time so much in need of protection.

Just for one moment he did not move and then his lips were on hers.

To Paola it was as if the Heavens opened

and the miracle she had prayed for enveloped her completely.

The terror which had shaken her whole body seemed to evaporate.

A warmth that might have been from the sun crept through her lips down into her breast.

The danger was past.

The *Marchese* was kissing her and it was Heaven to be in his arms.

It all happened so quickly.

Then while his lips held hers captive, there was the sudden explosion of other shots being fired in the adjacent room.

The *Marchese* raised his head.

"I must get you out of this!"

Paola could hardly understand what he was saying.

He set her on one side and walked across the room.

He picked up the blanket she had left lying beneath the arrow-slit and brought it to her.

He put his revolver in his pocket and, wrapping her in the blanket lifted her up in his arms.

She hid her face against his shoulder so that she did not see what had happened in the other room as they passed it.

The *Marchese* hurried along the passage

and down the steps to the entrance.

Outside the arched door his carriage was waiting.

There were several policemen beside it, but the *Marchese* ignored them.

He first put Paola inside the carriage and then joined her.

The Coachman, as if on his orders, drove off immediately.

As he did so the *Marchese* put his arm round Paola and drew her close to him.

"It is all over," he said, "and you have been very brave!"

"I was . . . frightened! Terribly . . . frightened that . . . you would not . . . understand."

"I understood," he said, "and I knew what agony you must be suffering. But when I came along the passage to where you were hidden, I had to wait until the door was open."

"And you . . . killed . . . him!" Paola murmured.

"He deserved to die. He has already committed a great number of murders, and his men killed two of our policemen."

"And . . . now at last . . . you are . . . safe from them," Paola murmured.

The *Marchese* thought that no other woman would be thinking of him at this moment rather than of herself.

"You saved me when you climbed up that appalling dirty chimney, and now I have saved you. I think we both have a great deal for which to be thankful."

"I . . . prayed and . . . prayed!" Paola said, "but . . . I was still . . . frightened that . . . you would . . . not understand."

"I understood," the *Marchese* said, "because you not only told me where you were in your letter, but I could hear you in my heart."

She looked up at him questioningly and he said:

"This is something that has never happened to me before. I could hear and understand what you were thinking just as I know now that I can read your thoughts."

Paola made a little murmur of surprise and he said:

"I think you know it already, but I will say it, to make quite certain that there is no mistake. I love you."

Paola's eyes seemed suddenly to be filled with sunshine.

Then as she looked up at him she turned her face and hid it against his shoulder.

"I want you to tell me," the *Marchese* said quietly, "what you feel for me."

He felt a little tremor run through her body.

He thought it was the most thrilling thing he had ever known.

His arm tightened as he said:

"Tell me my Darling, in words, what your eyes have told me already."

"I love . . . you," Paola whispered. "I cannot . . . help it, but I . . . love . . . you."

"That is all I want to know," the *Marchese* said.

He drove on in silence as if their minds were speaking to each other without words.

It was not long before they reached the Villa.

As they turned into the gates the *Marchese* said:

"I want you to go to bed and sleep as long as you can. We will talk about ourselves later today."

Without knowing really what she was saying, Paola answered:

"I do . . . not want to . . . leave . . . you."

"I have to go back," the *Marchese* said. "There are reports to be made and I want, if possible, to keep your name out of this. When it is finished, I too shall sleep. Then we have a great deal to talk about and to plan."

The carriage came to a standstill outside the front door.

Paola felt his lips on her forehead for a moment.

Then he was lifting her out of the carriage, and was carrying her upstairs to her Bedroom.

It was still very early but some servants were about obviously waiting for their return.

Without asking questions, Paola was certain that the *Contessa* had not been disturbed.

The *Marchese* laid her down on her bed.

As the maids came hurrying to attend to her he said quietly:

"Sleep well. There is no longer anything to make you afraid."

Then he was gone.

Paola washed her hands and face, got into bed and shut her eyes.

The *Marchese* had kissed her and said he loved her.

It was difficult to believe that she was not dreaming and that the nightmare of horror and fear was over.

He had saved her at the last moment when she feared he had forgotten her.

"I love . . . him. I love . . . him!" she said over and over again before she fell asleep.

When Paola woke, it was to find that it was luncheon time.

159

The maids were bringing her a meal on a tray.

"I have slept for a long time," she said.

"You must've been very tired, *Signorina,*" one of the maids said. "And the Master told us not to waken you 'til now!"

"And where is the *Contessa?*" Paola asked a little nervously.

She wondered what her hostess had been told, and thought she would be very perturbed by the horror of it.

She learnt, however, that the *Contessa* had gone back to her own Villa.

She would be returning later in the afternoon.

Paola gave a little sigh and started to eat what was waiting beside her.

When finally the maid brought her a cup of coffee, she said:

"The Master's downstairs, *Signorina,* and he asks you, if you feel well enough to join him."

Paola felt her heart leap.

The one thing she wanted was to see the *Marchese* alone.

The *Contessa* had gone home and was not expected back until later.

It was an opportunity which might not come again.

She jumped out of bed and the maids

helped her dress very quickly.

She put on one of her prettiest gowns and looked anxiously in the mirror when they arranged her hair.

The place where the Big Man had cut some away would not show.

'It will grow again,' she told herself.

At the same time, she wanted to look her best for the *Marchese.*

When she was ready she ran down the stairs.

A servant in the hall told her that the *Marchese* was not in the Drawing-Room but in his private Sitting-Room.

It was a little way along the corridor.

As Paola hurried there she thought it was somewhere where they would not be interrupted.

The footman opened the door for her.

She went in and heard it close behind her.

The *Marchese* was standing in front of the fireplace which, because it was summer, was filled with flowers.

The fragrance of the flowers was scenting the room.

For a moment neither of them moved.

Then the *Marchese* held out his arms.

Paola ran to him like a bird flying to shelter.

Then his lips were on hers and he was

kissing her demandingly, possessively.

At the same time, as if she was infinitely precious.

Only when they were both breathless did the *Marchese* raise his head and say in a voice that was unsteady:

"How can you make me feel like this?"

"Like . . . what?" Paola questioned.

"I know now," he said, "that I have never been in love before. This is love, my Darling. Love for an Angel, and what I feel is not human but Divine."

Then he was kissing her again until Paola felt her body melted completely into his and she was part of him.

They were no longer two people but one.

It was only with an effort that a little later the *Marchese* said:

"Now I have to talk to you, my Precious!"

As he spoke he drew her towards the sofa which was on one side of the fireplace.

He sat down, and put his arms round her.

For a moment he just looked at her before he said:

"How is it possible for you to be so beautiful, and at the same time so clever and so brave? There are no words to express my admiration for your courage."

Paola blushed.

"You are . . . making me feel . . . shy," she whispered.

"I adore you when you are shy," the *Marchese* said, "and that too makes you different from any other woman."

He bent his head for a moment as if he would kiss her again.

Then almost as if he pulled himself to attention he said:

"Now, what we have to decide, and it is important, is how soon will you marry me?"

Paola stared at him and then she said:

"Are you . . . really asking . . . me to . . . marry you? I always understood . . ."

". . . that I said I would never marry again," the *Marchese* added. "But you are mine, my Angel, and it is impossible for me to lose you."

Now he bent his head, but before his lips touched her, he said:

"We will be very, very happy. You can be quite certain of that."

It was impossible for Paola to speak or even to think because of the rapture his kiss gave her.

She felt as though the world had faded away and they were flying into the sky.

Only when the *Marchese* said in a voice that was deep and unsteady:

"You are not to tempt me until we have

sorted things out, and you have not yet told me if you will marry me."

"I find it . . . hard to . . . believe that . . . you are really asking . . . me. The *Contessa* told me that you never . . . made love to a . . . woman unless her . . . blood was as 'blue' as yours."

The *Marchese* laughed.

"That is true, but I think when it comes to an Angel, it is for you to criticise *my* blood."

Paola smiled and then she said:

"But suppose . . . when you get to . . . know the Angel well, you find her . . . like so many . . . other women who have been in your life — rather dull?"

She was teasing him, but at the same time her anxiety was genuine.

She could remember so many things the *Contessa* had said about the *Marchese*.

All of them had included again and again the warning that he went from one woman to another.

That he discarded them like flowers that had faded.

"I know exactly what you are thinking," the *Marchese* said, "and it is true, of course it is true. They were like faded flowers because they were not you."

"You are . . . reading my . . . thoughts," Paola accused him.

"As I have been able to do since I first knew you," the *Marchese* answered. "It has never happened to me with any other woman. That is why, my Darling, you are so very different, and it will take me a thousand years of loving you to tell you how different you are, and how much you mean to me."

He saw the love in Paola's eyes and he said:

"We will get married immediately. I want you! It is impossible for us to waste the precious hours and days when we might be close to each other."

His words brought Paola back to reality.

"I . . . love you," she said, "and though I know . . . very little . . . about love, I think I . . . love you as you . . . want to be loved. But I cannot . . . marry you for a . . . long time."

The *Marchese* stiffened.

"Why not?" he asked.

"I know that you truly love me because you have not asked me who I am," Paola said. "In fact the reason I have come to Lucca is that my Grandmother has died and I am in mourning for six months."

The *Marchese* stared at her and she said:

"I was to be a *débutante*. But of course that was now impossible, so I came out to Italy."

"Thank God for that," the *Marchese*

165

said, "or I might never have met you. But if we marry here in Italy surely we need not worry about your Grandmother?"

"Perhaps not, but I am afraid my Father and Mother will definitely disapprove of our . . . marriage," Paola said with difficulty.

"Disapprove?" the *Marchese* asked.

He looked at her in surprise.

She realised that it had never crossed his mind considering his position, that any woman would refuse to be his wife.

Nor that her Parents would disapprove.

"I do not understand," he said after a moment, "what you are saying."

Paola blushed and looked away from him.

"Please do not take offence if I tell you this," she said, "but when I came to . . . stay with the *Contessa*, she considered it . . . important that I should . . . not meet . . . you. It was arranged therefore that I should pretend to be Miss 'Nobody' so that . . . you would not . . . realise that we were distantly related."

"Related?" the *Marchese* said in astonishment. "But how?"

"My Mother's Grandmother was a member of your family," Paola said, "and she married an Englishman, the Duke of Ilchester."

166

"Of course I am aware of that," the *Marchese* said.

"Their daughter, my Grandmama," Paola continued, "is therefore half Italian and insisted on my learning that language when I was very small."

"And who is your Father?" the *Marchese* enquired.

"He is the Earl of Berisforde."

"I know him by name," the *Marchese* said, "and I think I have met him on several occasions at the Race Course."

"Papa was going to give a Ball for me in London," Paola went on, "and one in the country, but he agreed that I should come to Italy because it would be so disappointing to have to refuse every invitation until we were out of mourning."

"There is one invitation I have no intention of letting you refuse," the *Marchese* said, "and that is your Marriage to me."

Paola trembled.

Her eyes were worried as she said:

"I am terribly afraid that Papa . . . will oppose it, and I shall not be . . . allowed to . . . marry you."

"I assure you of one thing," the *Marchese* said. "You and I have been through deep waters together and fought against danger and evil in a way that happens to few people.

Do you really think, after that, we could allow anything to stand between us and our love?"

The way he spoke was very moving and Paola said:

"I love . . . you! I do love . . . you! But I feel sure Papa and Mama will at the . . . very least say that we have to wait . . . perhaps a year . . . in case you . . . change your mind. They will also do everything to try to find some other man for me to love as much as I love you."

The *Marchese* pulled her towards him.

"I swear to you, on everything I believe Holy, that I will not allow that to happen," he said furiously. "You are mine, Paola! Not only because you look like an Angel, but because St. Francis brought us together. I believe, as I believe in Heaven itself, that he helped us to save ourselves in situations which would have destroyed any other people."

"I am . . . sure that . . . is true," Paola agreed.

"Then what you have to do is to be very brave, and do what I ask you."

"What is . . . that?" Paola murmured.

She had a feeling it was going to be frightening.

"You will have to trust me," the *Mar-*

chese said, "when I tell you that my love for you is the love which comes from God. It has nothing to do with any emotions I have enjoyed with other women."

He looked at her and said:

"My Darling, you are so innocent and so unspoiled. You cannot expect me, having found the most precious pearl that has ever existed, to allow anyone else to handle it and to try to steal it from me."

Paola knew what he was saying.

At the same time she could only reply helplessly:

"What . . . can we . . . do?"

"I will tell you exactly what we are going to do. It may make your Father and Mother angry. But when they see how happy we are, and how we are made for each other by God, they will understand."

"What . . . will they . . . understand?" Paola asked.

"We are going to be married secretly," the *Marchese* replied. "And because it means so much to both of us, we will be married very early in the morning, before the Cathedral is open to the public, in the Chapel of St. Francis."

Paola gave a little gasp, but he went on:

"The Archbishop will perform the ceremony and I will ask him to keep it a complete and absolute secret, so that your Father will not be ashamed of his daughter marrying when she is in mourning."

He hesitated as if he was thinking it out before he continued:

"Our wedding will not be announced for at least six months. Then the English News-papers will be told that it took place in Lucca on whatever date we decide is most suitable."

He smiled as he added:

"A ceremony will take place again in the Chapel, but it will be one of Thanks-Giving because we are both so happy, and because we are thanking God for our having been man and wife for six months."

"How . . . can we . . . do . . . that?" Paola cried.

"Very easily," the *Marchese* said. "We will meanwhile tour the world. I want to show you Greece, the Pyramids, the Pearl Fishers in the Gulf, and perhaps the Hima-layas. We will not travel under my real name. I will use one of my minor titles, just to be sure we are comfortably looked after, but no-one will be particularly excited by who we are."

"H-how . . . can you . . . plan all . . . this?" Paola asked.

"I feel that the Saints and the Angels are

helping me," the *Marchese* answered. "You know exactly what I want. It is to be together and be sure of our love without really hurting the people who care for you."

"You are quite . . . sure that . . . no-one here will know what has . . . happened until we . . . come back?" Paola said.

It was difficult to grasp what he had said to her.

She was trying to understand.

But somehow it was difficult to think of anything but that he was close to her and she loved him.

She wanted him to kiss her again, giving her feelings which she never knew existed, but were, as he said, Divine.

"Now that is all decided," the *Marchese* said, "and, my Darling Angel you can just leave everything to me including the *Contessa*. All you have to do is to write letters to your Father and Mother."

He kissed her gently before he added:

"Explain to them how much we love each other and how under the circumstances it is impossible for us to wait to be joined together by God as man and wife. And I, of course, will write to them too."

"You are quite, quite . . . certain that what we are doing is . . . right?" Paola asked.

"I know it is right," the *Marchese* replied,

"because what would be wrong would be to allow doubts to spoil our rapture. The gossips and the cynics of this world would inevitably destroy the perfect love we have found by a miracle and which we must never lose."

He pulled her close to him as he said:

"Just leave it to me. I will arrange everything. My Darling Precious little Angel, all I want is that you should be mine, and that we should bring up our children in security and aware, as we have been, that we are specially protected by the Saints who look after us."

"That has . . . certainly happened . . . to us," Paola said.

"And it will go on happening," the *Marchese* promised. "Not just for a year, not even for our lifetime, but for all eternity."

Then he was kissing her again.

The *Contessa* came back just before tea-time and it was obvious she was very upset.

She was not only horrified at what had occurred.

Paola was aware that she was blaming the *Marchese* for what had happened.

In a somewhat cold voice she said:

"I went home so that I could see the Chief of Police, who promised he would guard my Villa carefully from now on."

No-one spoke and she continued:

"I understand that the men who took Paola away last night are now dead."

"That is true," the *Marchese* said, "so we shall have no more trouble from them. But I am sure you are right in taking no chances and if you are frightened, have your Villa guarded."

"Of course I am frightened," the *Contessa* snapped. "Who could imagine that anything like this in these days could happen in Lucca?"

She did not say so, but Paola was well aware she was implying it was the *Marchese*'s fault.

If he had not stirred up trouble, everything would have been calm and peaceful as it had been in the past.

Paola wanted to say something in his defence, but thought it would be a mistake.

The *Contessa* turned to her to say:

"My carriage is outside, Paola, and I suggest we go home now so that you can rest."

Paola looked despairingly at the *Marchese*.

But as she met his eyes she knew he was not worried and was telling her to trust him.

"I would like to thank the maid who has looked after me," Paola said humbly, "and as I have no money with me perhaps you would be kind enough to give me some."

"Yes, of course," the *Contessa* said.

She handed her two gold coins from her hand-bag.

Paola went upstairs.

She found that her clothes had already been packed and the maid was still in her Bedroom.

She thanked her and gave her the coins.

She bobbed a curtsy.

Paola put on her hat and picked up her hand-bag which had no money in it.

Then as she left the bedroom she found the *Marchese* outside.

He took her by the hand and pulled her across the corridor into an empty room on the other side.

"Listen, my Darling," he said. "Go back with the *Contessa* and say nothing. I will send you my instructions and all you have to do is to follow them."

"We cannot do what you propose," Paola said. "I love you . . . but you . . . know how . . . angry everyone will be if we get . . . married without anyone . . . knowing anything . . . about it. I cannot . . . imagine what the *Contessa* . . . will say to . . . Mama."

"At least we shall not be here to hear it," the *Marchese* said, "and once we are married nobody can separate us."

He could see that Paola was still indecisive.

Putting his arm around her, he lifted her chin with his other hand and tipped her face up to his.

"Listen, my Precious," he said. "Look into my eyes and tell me that you love me and that nothing else in the world is of any importance to either of us."

Because she could not help obeying him, Paola was lost.

"I love . . . you, I love . . . you," she whispered.

"And that is the only thing that matters," the *Marchese* said. "All you have to do my Darling is to rest and think of our love and believe that nothing and no-one will come between us."

He pulled her close to him and kissed her passionately.

Then because they both knew they were on dangerous ground, he took her to the door.

"Go downstairs and I will join you in a moment," he said. "It would be a great mistake to make the *Contessa* suspicious."

Swept away by the wonder of his kisses, it was difficult for Paola to think of anything except the ecstasy he evoked in her.

Yet she did as he told her.

She hurried downstairs and found the *Contessa* alone in the Drawing-Room.

"I am ready," Paola said as she entered.

"So I can see," the *Contessa* replied, "but our host seems to have disappeared."

Paola looked round as if she expected to see him somewhere else in the room.

While she was doing so he came in through the doorway.

"I am extremely sorry you must leave me," he said as he walked towards Paola, "but I do understand that after last night the *Contessa* feels that she must keep you with her."

"I promised her Mother that I would look after Paola and see that she did not get into trouble," the *Contessa* said.

As she said the last two words, she looked at the *Marchese*.

"I hope you will not worry her by telling her what has occurred," he urged. "After all it is something that could happen once in a million years."

"That is too often for me," the *Contessa* said. "Come along, Paola, the sooner we get home the better."

She swept out of the Drawing-Room and Paola looked at the *Marchese*.

His eyes were very soft as they rested on her troubled little face.

Then as she walked after the *Contessa* he joined her.

For a moment his hand held hers.

She felt the vibrations from him drawing her close.

She knew that despite what anybody might say or think, she was his completely.

Their love would conquer all the difficulties which lay ahead.

The *Contessa*'s carriage was waiting at the front door.

When Paola had been helped into it she bent forward to wave 'Goodbye' to the *Marchese.*

He was standing in the doorway, looking, she thought, as if not only the beautiful Villa, but the whole world belonged to him.

Only as the carriage moved away down the drive did she wonder frantically if she was leaving her heart behind.

Now she was gone he might forget her.

Then she remembered he had asked her to trust him, and that was what she must do.

They could not let the love they had for each other be spoilt by other people, no matter what they might think.

The carriage had hardly passed through the gates before the *Contessa* said:

"I do not know what your Mother will think now that you have become involved with the one man in the whole of Lucca of whom she disapproves."

"I think Mama and Papa would understand it is not the *Marchese*'s fault," Paola replied.

"Then who else?" the *Contessa* asked sharply. "Who else would have murderers following him from the East and kidnapping you who had nothing to do with him?"

She paused then added scornfully:

"You should not have been in his Villa at all!"

"He only took us there because he thought we would be safe," Paola said.

The *Contessa* gave a sharp laugh.

"Safe?" she exclaimed. "With you spirited away in the middle of the night, and of all places taken to the Watch-Tower. As I said to the Chief of Police, it is a disgrace to the City that this should happen, that is what it is."

"I am sure the *Marchese* is hoping that only very few people will know about it," Paola said weakly.

"That is just what the Police said to me," the *Contessa* answered. "But I cannot believe that anything so outrageous and extraordinary can be kept a secret."

"I am sure the *Marchese* will not mention it," Paola murmured, "and you would not want anyone to know how I was involved."

She knew as she spoke that she had played a trump card.

The *Contessa* lapsed into silence.

It was only a short distance to her Villa.

When they arrived the *Contessa* suggested that Paola should go up to her Bedroom and lie down.

"Better still go to bed," she said. "There is no point in your getting up for dinner this evening, and I must say you are looking very pale and there are lines underneath your eyes."

Paola hoped that the *Marchese* had not noticed them and did not think she looked plain.

When she reached her Bedroom she ran to the mirror.

Although it was true she looked slightly pale she could not see any lines.

Anyway because she was thinking of him her eyes were shining.

She was however quite ready to lie down or to go to bed so that she could think.

She wanted to go over quietly what the *Marchese* had proposed they should do.

Now when she thought it over it seemed utterly and completely impossible.

How could she get married in Lucca in secret without making her Father and

Mother aware of it?

Whatever the *Marchese* might say, she was sure it was wrong.

Then she told herself:

"The *Marchese* is quite right. If we have to wait for six months with everyone telling me he is raffish, a roué, and will eventually leave me as he has left so many other women, what chance have we of real happiness?"

She had already heard before she met him how everyone discussed everything he did!

While they enjoyed repeating stories of his love-affairs, they were not thinking of his point of view.

"He truly loves me," Paola assured herself.

She remembered how he had said she was different from anyone else he had ever known.

How they were aware of each other's thoughts.

'I know,' Paola told herself, 'I could never feel the same with another man. I could never love anyone else in the same way.'

Then she added:

'Apart from anything else it would be impossible to find another man who is so outstanding. Not only being so handsome but also with so strong a personality.'

He had been so calm and unflurried in the desperate situation in which they had found themselves that she had managed to follow his example.

She knew when he said he had prayed that was the truth.

She could not imagine herself talking in the same way to an Englishman.

Nor would any Englishman have said the things to her that the *Marchese* had said.

'He is a man who believes in God,' she thought 'and that is more important than anything else.'

As time passed, she felt very lonely.

It was so wonderful to know that the *Marchese* was near and that everything in his Villa was a part of him.

Then almost as if she was being tempted into unhappiness, she seemed to hear a little voice.

It was whispering that now she had left, he might be thinking of someone else.

Perhaps he was planning to go back to Florence rather than carry out with her all the wild plans he had suggested.

"I love . . . him, I love . . . him," she murmured over and over again.

There was a knock on the door.

The maid came in with a beautiful basket of flowers.

The flowers were all white and the basket was ornamented with white satin ribbon.

"With the compliments of *Signore the Marchese di Lucca*," the maid said, and put it down beside the bed.

Paola waited until the maid had left her.

Then instinctively, almost as if Vittorio was speaking to her, she looked amongst the flowers.

Amongst them, as she had hoped, was a note.

She pulled it out eagerly.

She opened it and read:

'I love you, I love you, my beautiful wife to be. Trust me and do not be afraid. St. Francis and the Angels are with us and we cannot fail.
Yours adoringly, Vittorio.'

His words gave her so much happiness that Paola felt the tears come into her eyes.

Then she kissed his letter, feeling that was what he had done before he sent it.

A little later she fell asleep and was still sleeping when dinner was brought to her.

She sat up and ate it and when she had finished the *Contessa* came to her room.

182

"I hear you have been asleep Paola," she said. "That is the best thing that could happen to you."

"I am sorry you had to dine alone," Paola said politely.

The *Contessa* was not listening but looking at the basket of flowers.

"At least he has very good manners," she said. "And you certainly deserve flowers after all you have been through."

"I am trying to forget about it," Paola said. "Please do not mention it when you write to Mama. It would only worry her."

"I suppose I should tell her if I did my duty," the *Contessa* replied. "But I do not want her to worry about you while you are with me, and so we will neither of us say anything."

That was exactly what Paola wanted.

"Now I am quite safe here with you," she said.

"I sincerely hope so," the *Contessa* replied a little doubtfully.

Paola thought she was about to say something more.

But she obviously changed her mind.

However, she glanced rather meaningfully at the basket of flowers before she left the room.

Paola thought she could understand what

the *Contessa* was feeling.

After all, she had been told the one man her protégé, while staying with her in Lucca, was not to meet or to have any contact with was the *Marchese*.

Who would have imagined, who would have thought for one moment that such things would happen?

Just because Hugo had asked her to carry a diamond ring secretly to Lucca.

Now in retrospect it all seemed so absurd that she gave a little laugh.

Then she cuddled down comfortably in the bed.

She put the *Marchese*'s letter under her pillow so that she could touch it.

Paola awoke the following morning to find it was far later than she usually awakened.

Her breakfast was brought to her in bed.

"You are spoiling me," she said when the *Contessa* came to see her a little later.

"One often suffers from shock when one has had an experience such as you have had," the *Contessa* replied.

"As I have several things to do this morning, I suggest you stay in bed until luncheon."

Paola did as she was told.

When later she came downstairs, she found to her relief that the *Contessa* had one of her friends to luncheon.

She was helping her arrange a Concert to be held later in the year in aid of the Cathedral.

They had so much to talk about that Paola could be silent and unnoticed, which was what she wanted.

After they had eaten, the *Contessa* suggested to Paola that she should take a book and read it in the garden.

"Or better still," she suggested, "doze while it is so hot."

Paola did not argue but went into the garden.

The *Contessa* had an appointment with someone else who was also to help with the Concert.

Paola had not been alone long when a manservant announced, *'The Marchese di Lucca.'*

Paola looked up and felt her heart turn a somersault as he came in, looking as usual so overwhelmingly handsome.

She just wanted to stare at him.

He sat down beside her and lifted her hand to his lips.

He kissed each finger and then pressed a long and passionate kiss in the palm.

Paola felt as if the world was swinging dizzily round her.

She could only look at him, her eyes filling her whole small face.

"How are you, my Darling?" the *Marchese* asked. "I missed you last night and it was agony this morning to know you were not in my Villa, even though not far away from me."

"I missed you too," Paola said, "and thank you for your lovely flowers and your letter."

"I hoped I would be able to see you alone and tell you what I want to do," the *Marchese* said.

Paola felt herself stiffen for a moment.

Then as if she could not help it, she felt as if her whole being moved towards him.

She was ready to do anything he wished, anything he asked of her.

"I cannot trust servants," he began, "not to talk and thus alert the *Contessa* to stop you doing what I want. So I have brought you something quite new — an alarm-clock."

"I have heard of them but I have never seen them," Paola said.

The *Marchese* brought one from his pocket.

It was not very large, but when he pressed

a little knob at the back it made a sound like the ringing of bells.

"That is fascinating!" she exclaimed.

"I am going to set it," he said, "for half-past six tomorrow morning. It will wake you and you alone, and I suppose you can dress yourself?"

"Of course I can," Paola laughed. "You do not suppose I had servants to dress me when I was at school!"

"I want you to wear a white gown," he said, "and to slip out of the house by the side entrance. You know where it is?"

"Yes, of course," Paola said. "No-one will see me if I leave that way."

"That is what I thought," the *Marchese* said. "I shall be waiting for you in a closed carriage. I will have with me a veil for you to wear over your head and a wreath of flowers to hold it in place."

He smiled before he said:

"You will also have a bouquet, my Darling, to make you feel like a proper Bride."

"Are . . . we really going . . . to be . . . married?" Paola asked in a small voice.

"Really and truly," he said, "so that I will never lose you again, or you me."

"That is . . . what I am . . . afraid may happen," Paola murmured.

"I know that," he answered. "There are a

great number of people ready to tell you what a bad husband I will make, and that might perhaps spoil our love for each other."

Paola did not speak. Then after a moment he said:

"I swear to you on my immortal soul and everything I hold sacred that I will love you, look after you and worship you as my wife, as long as we live."

He spoke with such sincerity that Paola knew she had to believe him.

She knew too he was right in saying that if anyone else learnt what they were about to do they would try to stop her.

She was very young and they would be sure the *Marchese* would make her an exceedingly bad husband.

But every instinct in her body told her they were wrong.

When his heart talked to her heart, she knew it was the truth.

"When you join me tomorrow morning," the *Marchese* was saying, "you leave everything to me. I have been planning to make our honeymoon, my beautiful one, the most perfect one there has ever been."

"I just . . . want to be . . . with you," Paola said because she could not help herself.

"That is what I want too," he answered.

He hesitated as if feeling for words before he said:

"There is something I want you to remember and something we shall both think of year after year."

"What is that?" Paola asked.

"We will know how right we were to run away from everything that tried to spoil the perfection we found together."

When he finished speaking he bent forward and kissed her.

It was a very gentle kiss.

Paola knew it was one of dedication, and what he had said had come from his heart and soul and not just from his lips.

He rose to his feet.

"You are . . . not leaving . . . me?" Paola asked.

"I am going away, my Darling, because I have so much to do. But I shall be thinking of you and, if you are thinking of me, we shall be very close as we have been since we first met."

Paola smiled.

"I was thinking just now how . . . extraordinary it was that when those . . . terrible things happened to us we were both quite . . . calm and . . . certain that . . . everything would come . . . right. That was the . . . feeling . . . you gave . . . me."

"In finding you," the *Marchese* answered, "I found the woman for whom I was always seeking, although I was not aware of it. But with you I have discovered real true love which I thought only existed in Heaven."

Paola held on to his hand.

"You will . . . not forget . . . me?"

The *Marchese* smiled.

"You fill my whole thoughts, my whole world," he said, "and after tomorrow we will never be apart."

Once again he kissed her hand.

Then he went quickly before she could think of anything else to say.

When he had gone she realised how happy he made her.

Now the last doubts had disappeared and she could only wait impatiently until tomorrow.

The little alarm tinkled, but as it happened Paola was already awake.

She had put everything ready the night before.

Now she jumped out of bed, washed in cold water and dressed herself as quickly as she could.

She had laid out the very prettiest of her white gowns.

Only then did she ask herself what she was to do about other clothes.

The *Marchese* had not mentioned it.

She thought she could hardly go away with him on her honeymoon with only one gown.

Then she told herself that if she had forgotten he quite certainly had not.

He would either spirit some clothes to her or perhaps buy them where they were going.

The only thing that mattered this morning was that she should be married to him as he was planning.

After that everything in her life would have changed completely.

When she drew back the curtains she had seen it was a perfect day.

The sun was just climbing up in the sky.

The birds were singing in the trees and there was the soft buzz of the bees in the flowers growing up the wall outside the window.

She had a little difficulty in doing up her dress at the back, but somehow she managed it.

Then picking up her handkerchief to carry with her, she very cautiously opened the door of her Bedroom.

No-one in the house was yet moving.

The servants were all old.

They saw no reason to rise early unless there was some urgent need for it.

Paola tip-toed down the stairs and out through the garden door.

It was bolted on the inside.

She drew the bolts back very cautiously, afraid she might wake anyone.

Then she was in the garden moving swiftly behind the shrubs and trees.

She reached the side gate into the Villa.

As it came in sight, she saw the closed carriage waiting outside.

She knew with a feeling of wild excitement that the *Marchese* was there for her.

He got out of the carriage to help her in.

They did not speak, but just looked at each other.

She had forgotten that he would be wearing evening-dress as was correct on the Continent.

She thought it became him more than anything else he wore.

As the carriage drove off the *Marchese* put his arm around Paola.

She could think of nothing but the nearness of him and the love which seemed to swell like a tidal wave within her breasts.

"You have come, my Precious one," the *Marchese* said. "I was half afraid that at the last moment you would not be brave enough to do so."

"I had to . . . come because . . . you wanted . . . me," Paola said.

"And that is the right answer," he replied. "I shall always want you."

He did not kiss her, but picked up an exquisite veil which was on the seat opposite them.

He put it on her head.

Then placed on top of it a wreath of white roses.

It was very skilfully made and fitted exactly.

On the small seat was her bouquet which was also of white roses.

Almost as if she had asked the question, he said:

"That is what you are to me, a white rosebud, my Precious, not yet in full blossom."

He finished arranging her wreath as he spoke and Paola said:

"Do . . . I look . . . all right?"

"You look so beautiful that I am afraid to touch you," the *Marchese* said. "You might have stepped down from Heaven itself."

His lips just touched her hand which he was holding in his and they drove on in silence.

It was only a short distance to the Cathedral.

They stopped by a side door which was opened for them by a Verger.

When they entered Paola was conscious of the intense atmosphere of faith.

It was what she had felt the first time she entered the Cathedral.

Now there was also the scent of incense and the fragrance of flowers.

When they reached the Chapel of St. Francis Paola saw that the whole Altar was decorated with white roses.

The Archbishop was waiting for them wearing a white vestment.

The candles were all lit.

There were two servers, men not boys, and no-one else.

Paola had heard the marriage service read many times, but she thought it had never been spoken with more sincerity.

She felt that God was blessing both her and the *Marchese* as they knelt before the Archbishop.

Having blessed them he turned away to kneel in prayer at the Altar.

Then the *Marchese* took Paola by the hand and drew her to her feet.

They moved out of the Chapel and left the Cathedral by the same side door.

The carriage was waiting and drove swiftly away.

It was not far to the *Marchese*'s Villa.

When they reached it the sunshine had only just begun to glitter on the windows and on the fountains playing in the garden.

They had both been so deeply moved by the service in which they had just taken part that neither of them had spoken since they left the Cathedral.

But now as they went in through the main door the Major Domo bowed and said:

"May I, most honoured *Marchese,* congratulate you and your lady wife and wish you every happiness in the future."

"You are the only person, Antonio," the *Marchese* said, "who knows we are married, and you must keep it to yourself for a long time. We will leave as soon as we have changed."

"Everything is arranged," the Major replied.

Taking Paola by the hand, the *Marchese* took her up the stairs.

Only as she reached the top did she ask:

"Where are we going?"

"On our Honeymoon," he answered. "First we have to change. The clothes I bought for you are waiting."

Paola looked at him in surprise and then she laughed.

"I knew you would think of it."

"I think of you, and nothing else is of any importance," the *Marchese* replied.

He showed her into an exquisitely beautiful Bedroom.

Paola thought it must have been used by the previous *Marchesa di Lucca*.

There were white roses everywhere.

Laid out on the carved and gilded bed was a very smart travelling gown and a cloak.

There was also an attractive bonnet to match the blue of the gown.

She took off her wedding gown and put on the one he had bought for her.

She was not surprised it fitted exactly and thought only he could be so clever.

Not only to remember what she would want but to find it at such short notice.

She was just putting the finishing touches to her bonnet when he came to the door saying:

"Are you ready?"

He had changed into comfortable driving clothes.

He looked even more distinguished in them she thought, than he had in the evening-dress he had worn to be married.

He held out his hand.

She ran to slip hers into it and they went down the stairs side by side.

Only as they were driving away in a comfortable open Chaise drawn by four white horses did Paola manage to ask where they were going.

"As far as I am concerned, to Heaven," the *Marchese* replied. "And now my Darling, my Sweet and perfect little wife, I need not feel afraid that something might happen to prevent us becoming as we are now — man and wife."

"It is so . . . wonderful I do not . . . believe it is . . . true," Paola said.

"That is what I am feeling," he answered. "When we arrive where no-one can interrupt us, I will tell you all the things I have been wanting to tell you and for which there has never been enough time."

Paola laughed.

"That is true! So many things have happened so quickly it has almost been difficult to breathe."

She drew a big breath as if to make sure she could and then said:

"Before we say any more, you must tell me what you have done about Papa and Mama, and the *Contessa*."

"I have written to your Father and Mother," the *Marchese* replied, "and explained exactly why we have run away and that there will be no scandal about our marriage as long as it is kept a secret."

"I hope Papa will do that," Paola murmured.

"I am sure if they are sensible people they will understand and say nothing until your mourning is over."

Paola gave a little sigh of relief.

"I also told your parents," the *Marchese* went on, "that the *Contessa* is trusted on her honour not to say anything in Lucca. I have enclosed to her a copy of the letter I sent to your Father and Mother. I am quite certain that will ensure she will say nothing even to her closest friends."

Paola clasped her hands together.

"You are splendid! You are wonderful!" she exclaimed. "Only you could do anything so outrageous as marrying me in secret and still get away with it."

"Touch wood," the *Marchese* said. "I am certain we are safe and the only other two people who know about us are the Archbishop and my Major Domo, who has been with me since I was a small boy, and who would rather die than hurt me in any way."

Paola was sure all the people who worked for him felt the same.

She was so relieved at what he had told

her that she felt her last doubts and fears slip away.

"Now," the *Marchese* was saying, "I will tell you where we are going. It is to Bagni di Lucca where I have a small Castle. I think you will find it enchanting. I have always thought since I was a child that it is a fairy Castle."

He drove on a little further before he added:

"I want you to know I have never been there with any other woman. It is also some years since I visited it, so I know how pleased they will be to see us when we arrive."

They had not very far to go.

When they arrived before luncheon Paola thought she had never seen anything so lovely as Bagni di Lucca.

The River Lima flowed slowly through small hamlets situated on its banks.

The hills and mountains rose above it bringing in, the *Marchese* told her, since the Middle Ages, health-giving properties.

This was verified by documents dating back to the 11th century.

When Paola saw the Castle she knew it really was like a fairy tale.

As they drove up to it she could see there was something about it which, like everything to do with the *Marchese* was different.

It was not the mellow grey stonework of the building or the exquisitely beautiful flower-gardens which surrounded it.

There was an atmosphere encompassing it as if it had been made for love.

The servants waiting for them were all very old. They had served in the *Marchese*'s family since he had been born.

They were obviously thrilled and delighted to be allowed to be a part of his honeymoon.

They had decorated the house with flowers including, on his instructions, a great number of white rose buds.

Everything was perfect.

Paola was therefore not surprised when she went up into the large Bedroom to find there were clothes for her in the wardrobe.

There were white roses by the bed and on the dressing table.

When she had washed she went downstairs where luncheon was waiting.

The Dining-Room had a mediaeval charm about it.

It seemed to her appropriate that the *Marchese* was sitting in a high-backed carved armchair which made him look, she thought, like a King.

The food was delicious, but it was difficult to think about anything except that she
was his wife.

She had run away with the most re-
nowned and talked-about man in Italy and
it was not just a story!

"I think I am dreaming," Paola said
before the meal was finished.

"I am quite certain I am," the *Marchese*
answered. "But I have never been so happy
in the whole of my life or so completely and
absolutely certain that I have done the right
thing."

"Oh! Please go on . . . thinking that and
. . . never have any . . . doubts," Paola
pleaded.

"Do you think it is possible I should?" he
enquired.

He did not wait for an answer but drew
her from the table.

She thought he was going to show her
some of the Castle.

Instead they went upstairs into the room
where she had left her cape and bonnet.

"Because we have risen very early," he
said, "we are now going to have, which is a
regular habit in this country, a Siesta."

Paola looked at him wide-eyed and he
said:

"My Darling, my Sweet, you do not suppose I can wait any longer to tell you of my love and to teach you to love me?"

Very gently he undid her gown.

When it fell to the ground he lifted her up in his arms and carried her into the huge golden canopied bed.

He laid her down on the pillows.

The sunshine came through the window and there was the sound of the birds outside.

Paola thought once again she was dreaming and this could not be true.

The *Marchese* joined her.

He put his arm around her and drew her close to him.

Although her lips were waiting, for the moment he did not kiss her.

Her eyes were looking up to his and after a moment he said:

"I was thanking God that I have found you and that in so strange and unusual a manner we have been brought together as we were meant to be since the very beginning of time."

"And no-one . . . will ever . . . part us?" Paola asked.

She was not for the moment thinking of her parents.

But of the men who tried to kill the *Marchese* for the diamond ring and who themselves had perished.

"There was something I was going to tell you," the *Marchese* said, as he knew what she was thinking.

"There will . . . not be . . . others?" Paola questioned nervously.

He shook his head.

"Yesterday I sent the money I promised to Hugo Forde and the ring to His Holiness the Pope. I asked him either to put it with the treasures in the Vatican or to sell it and give the proceeds to be distributed in the name of St. Francis of Assisi to those who are in need."

Paola gave a little cry.

"I am . . . glad about that . . . so very glad. Now it will . . . no longer . . . menace us."

"I have no intention of ever thinking of it again," the *Marchese* said. "It served its purpose in bringing us together and now everything that is ugly and cruel and evil must be kept from you. That is what I must spend the rest of my life doing."

His arms tightened.

"You are so beautiful, so pure and unspoilt," he said. "I will show you in the Library what Lord Byron and Shelley wrote about this magical place and I feel the same."

Paola looked at him in surprise and he said very softly:

"Seeking love I travelled far and wide,
But the blossoms I picked faded and
died,
Disillusioned, I swore no love was
true,
Then an Angel from Heaven came — it
was you!
Beautiful, perfect, your heart beats
with mine,
You have taught me my Darling, that
love is Divine."

Paola gave a little cry.

"Oh Darling you wrote that for me? It is so clever of you!"

"Not quite Lord Byron," the *Marchese* said, "but it is yours with my heart."

He drew her close to him and his lips sought hers.

Just before he kissed her she prevented him from doing so and said:

"There is . . . something I . . . want to . . . ask you."

"What is it?" the *Marchese* enquired.

"You know I . . . am very . . . ignorant about . . . love," she said. "Will you . . . teach me to . . . love you as you . . . want to be loved, so that I will . . . never disappoint . . . you?"

There was a tender expression in the *Mar-*

204

chese's eyes that no-one had ever seen before as he said:

"I will teach you about love, my beautiful one, and it will be the real love which comes from God. A love which saved us when you were in danger and which made us realise we belonged to each other and could not go on living alone."

He kissed her forehead very gently before he went on:

"It is a love which has brought us here to a new world where no-one will disturb us until we are completely one person and it is a love which will make us that."

As he finished speaking he kissed Paola at first very gently.

Then as he felt her body move closer to him, his kisses became more possessive and more passionate.

Paola felt an ecstasy which she never knew existed and which responded to the same feeling in the *Marchese*.

He went on kissing and kissing her.

She felt as if there were little sparks of fire within her heart and her soul.

In a strange way they responded to a fire burning within him.

Yet at the same time they were all part of the wonder and beauty of love.

It was like a light from Heaven which involved them completely.

It came too from their hearts and souls, and also from their minds.

It was the light and love of God which was theirs.

They would never lose it and as the *Marchese* made Paola his she knew it would be theirs for all Eternity.

We hope you have enjoyed this Large Print book. Other Thorndike, Wheeler or Chivers Press Large Print books are available at your library or directly from the publishers.

For more information about current and upcoming titles, please call or write, without obligation, to:

Publisher
Thorndike Press
295 Kennedy Memorial Drive
Waterville, ME 04901
Tel. (800) 223-1244

Or visit our Web site at:
www.thomson.com/thorndike
www.thomson.com/wheeler

OR

Chivers Large Print
published by BBC Audiobooks Ltd
St James House, The Square
Lower Bristol Road
Bath BA2 3BH
England
Tel. +44(0) 800 136919
email: bbcaudiobooks@bbc.co.uk
www.bbcaudiobooks.co.uk

All our Large Print titles are designed for easy reading, and all our books are made to last.

n6
3/07

cB
8/07

ML

9/06